ISMENE

THE
JOURNEY BACK

CHRISTINE
EMMERT

PUBLISH
AMERICA

PublishAmerica
Baltimore

First printing

ISBN: 1-4137-9804-7
PUBLISHED BY PUBLISHAMERICA, LLLP
www.publishamerica.com
Baltimore

Printed in the United States of America

*With thanks to Zoe,
who helped me with Ismene's journey…*

Acknowledgments

No writer produces work in the manner of a hermit. I have many people to thank for this novel. My husband, Richard, and my son, Alex, have been the most important influences in my life and constantly inspire me with their observations, critical suggestions, and unflagging support. They are my heart and blood and spirit.

Zoe Chambers was person with whom I did the first figurings of this story as a one-act play with herself as Ismene and myself as Tieresias. It is Zoe's face I saw when I took my little offering and expanded it into a novel. In this regard, I must also acknowledge Faylee Favara, who put on the evening where the play was performed. And Jenny MacDonald who asked innocently afterwards if there was, perhaps, a novel in the works.

My many friends have been a source of strength for me—Renee Cafiero, Stephanie Cowell, Salle Tulchin, Marty and Stan Meyers, Shirley Michaels, Todd Misk, and more. A newer friend, and one equally important, is Venda Peterson, my son's soul mate.

In addition, I appreciate the love my sister, Barbara Casini, has given me across this long, hard journey of life.

I am indebted to Joseph Campbell for his book, *Hero of a Thousand Faces*, which helped me define how a person transforms their life. He suggested the map for Ismene's story when he set forth the evolutionary road of the hero/heroine.

On self-sprung wings
I took my flight
Through the skies
Of my own history....

fragment of a song by Orpheus

PROLOGUE

Weeping. She could hear the sound from her hiding-place. Then running. Finally the scream of her nurse. More footsteps. She came out slowly, walking down the hall towards her parents' bedchamber.

Her father was there, reaching upwards. Following the progress of his arm, she saw first her mother's feet, then body, and head. her mother hung from a beam of ceiling by a braided scarlet thread. In a moment of strength—a cry escaping from his lips—her father pulled the body free.

"Father?" she spoke softly. He was tugging at the pins of her mother's gown. "Father?"

"Ismene!" Her father spun around to face her, the pins in his grip. " Go!"

She moved a step closer, but something about her father's face stopped her from touching him.

"Ismene..." His voice was gentle now. "You are the last person I will ever look upon." Slowly he took the pins, one in each hand, and pressed them into his eyes.

Ismene turned, running until she found the coolest part of the garden by the high wall. Reaching down, she scooped water from a puddle, rubbing it into her hot skin. Then she closed her eyes, screaming until her nurse came to find her.

PART ONE: DESCENT

The fire rose up, a dangerous animal, within the cave. The girl drew back until the gradual retreat of flame.

"Will it be better now?" she asked the shadowy figure sitting unmoved before the fury of the fire.

"For a time," the figure said after deliberation.

The girl, shivering, came closer to the source of heat. Her clothing was soaked from the rains outside. "I am cold, Tieresias."

Take off your wrappings," the figure suggested. "You will warm faster without those dripping garments." When she hesitated, Tieresias smiled, adding, "I cannot see you."

Ismene laughed. "I forgot. Sometimes I think you see everything."

Tieresias shrugged: "Everything and nothing."

Standing naked, warming under the ministrations of the flame's fingers, Ismene rubbed her numb limbs. She was delighting in her tingling return to comfort.

"I want to stay here with you, Tieresias," she announced. "There is no one left for me in Thebes."

"Your uncle…"

"My uncle will kill me, if he can. He hates me and all my flesh. They are gone now. I am the last to be destroyed. When I am dead, there will be none to challenge him."

"I will still be here," the voice spoke slowly and distinctly.

"He does not believe you are his enemy."

"I am not his enemy, but I will tell him the truth. He may not like what I will say."

There was a small pause, and then Ismene asked in her soft voice, "May I stay here? I could be useful to you."

"You are a young girl. What would you do here in a cave with a blind prophet?"

"What should I do in the world? I lived in the Palace, constantly stared at and gossiped about by the people. No man would ever make me an offer of marriage who knows the curse placed on my family. My sister, Antigone, was my only friend. Creon killed her. My old nurse died the next day of a broken heart. If you turn me away...," she stopped to ease the desperation in her voice. Tears were held back. Once, Tieresias had said tears were the most potent weapons of the weak.

As though the words stirred the prophet, the figure arose, pacing back and forth on the other side of the fire. Finally, Tieresias said, "Creon will not let me keep you here. He will send his guards."

"How will he know?"

"He knows already. His spies must have followed you, turning back after you climbed this cliff. Creon's mind is turning on how to retrieve you without angering me."

Ismene moved quickly to Tieresias's side, touching the prophet's hand with hers. On her touch, the prophet moved away, but Ismene persisted, "You must give him word that to remove me would anger you. He is afraid of you."

Tieresias's face made no shift in expression. The old hand, like a claw, gathered in her own and pressed hard. She tried not to cry out.

"Why me, Ismene?"

"You seem familiar. Much like my father. It is the absence of your eyes. He gave up his eyes for a vision. I was with him at Colonus. Not just Antigone. I led him into the sacred grove. In the end, he was not a tragic man."

The old hand relented. Her skin was bruised where his hand had pressed into her.

Treresias sighed, "None of what happened was your father's fault. Nor was it your mother's."

"I know…"

"You seem familiar as well, Ismene." Tieresias touched her cheek in a surprisingly gentle gesture. "Your voice, your skin, the smell of you reminds me of my own youth."

"May I stay?"

"Just through tonight. Tomorrow, you must leave."

She took hope from this small yielding, "I can cook for you tonight. I can recite."

The prophet moved away, around the fire. "There is a robe I used to wear over by the cave's entrance. Put on that robe."

With some delay, she went to the entrance, finding the garment folded neatly on a rocky ledge. The fit was perfect.

"When did you first wear this robe, Tieresias?"

The voice became shy, "When I was a maiden. I wore it the first night of love I experienced."

"It fits me well."

"I know. You look beautiful."

"You cannot see me," she protested.

"Not with my eyes, but…," the sentence was left unfinished. "There is wine in the jug on the ledge by the garment. Pour some for us. We have to decide where you should go…."

Ismene, dressed in the blue of a maiden, laughed, "Everything is easy with you."

"You do not know where I am sending you," the prophet admonished her.

* * *

The river rushed past. Tieresias had described this particular river as "wine-swollen." The dark purple waters left no room for doubt. This river was the one he had directed her towards. She stood on the bank watching the sun deposit the last spill of daylight. Her own pulse raced with the water, although her body was tired. The journey had been a long one, often misdirected from a hastily drawn map she had made in the cave at Tieresias's terse bidding.

11

No real river ever looked as angry as the one before her, flowing out of myth. Styx was a boundary where, once crossed, few returned. Her own mother told her the story of the gnarled ferryman, the descent into the earth that lay on the other side, and the three-headed dog who would not let the living pass.

"Only the dead are welcome there," Tieresias told her." You will be safe from Creon's soldiers. You must ask all the questions you have, but accept, as well, the answers given."

"Then I can return?" Ismene gave voice to her wish.

"Then you can return, if you still wish to live out your life on this earth."

It was in that brief moment she realized how much she loved the earth.

"I will go there," she assented. "Will I see my family?"

"All your family. Some never seen by you on this side of the Styx."

Her memory drew the faces of her two proud brothers, her sister, who always seemed in a rage, and her parents. It was the recollection of her mother's face that prompted tears. The face ringed gentleness within a tragic contour.

"Your mother will not look the same to you in Hades. She is free there to smile."

"I am not accustomed to my mother's smile."

"Take this flask with you. It contains a potion to help you see." The old hand thrust a small flask towards her.

"I can see. I have my eyes."

"Only outer eyes. This potion gives you inner sight."

When she left, the prophet was perched on the ledge like a wise old bird.

"You will come back to me, Ismene, if you are able," came the prophet's voice

"I thank you." Ismene embraced the wizened figure. "We will meet again."

She went running down the cliff, her desire to laugh aloud stifled in respect for this old blind figure who stood at the cliff's pinnacle.

Now she waited at the river's edge. The sun had surrendered to the night. Apollo's chariot would be placed in the heavenly stable.

The goddess, Artemis, would take her place in the sky, floating in her silvery disc, attended by a court of stars.

"Such a night!" A voice spoke close to her. Ismene gave a sharp intake of breath. She had thought herself alone on the river bank. The voice was low-pitched but female. Turning, Ismene took sight of a woman dressed royally as any queen. The woman did not look unfriendly.

"Such a night," Ismene echoed with a slight inclination of her head. What brought such a woman to this place at this time?

"Soon it will warm. There is a kinder moon shining already." The woman raised one glorious arm in gesture towards the heavens.

"Are you dead?" Ismene voiced her reluctant thought.

"No, my child. I cannot die. My diet is ambrosia and nectar. I might ask if you are dead."

"I must think of myself as such."

"Then you are intending to cross the river?"

"Oh yes. I hope soon. There are those behind me who would like me to return with them."

The woman made no comment. For a long second, they listened together to the churning of the water.

"Do you hear the ferryman?" the woman asked at last. Ismene could hear a baritone voice intoning over the music of the Styx.

"Will you cross the river as well?" she asked the woman.

"Ah no. I am waiting for my daughter. He brings her to me each year at this time."

"But how can that be? Those who cross cannot come back, except...," Ismene stopped. She looked at the face of this woman under full glow of the moon. The woman's eyes burned gold.

"Forgive me." Ismene bent her head. "I did not recognize you, Demeter."

"And why should a mortal recognize a goddess?" The woman gave a light laugh. "Yes, it is my daughter, stolen from me by Hades, who comes back to me now. Just for six months. Then he claims her again."

The sound of the man's voice grew closer. Ismene heard the splashing of oars. A moment later, a slender girl appeared. She was drenched in silver, shimmering as she moved.

"Mother!" the voice was hopeful.

"Perserphone, I am here." The goddess and her daughter embraced, then quickly passed Ismene, swallowed up in the night.

Ismene stood still, uncertain how to proceed.

"Is there a passenger?" the man's voice rang out.

To go into the kingdom of death! Without the protection of a goddess! Ismene paused a moment.

"Is there a passenger?"

"Yes, I am a passenger." Ismene stepped closer to the shore. She saw the boat and the presence of Charon, whose responsibility it was to take the dead to their new home.

"You are not dead, my daughter." Charon gestured her back.

"For a time, I must be dead. Tieresias has commanded me to come here."

"Tieresias…," Charon reflected on the name. "How is the old scoundrel? Which sex is our prophet these days?"

Although Ismene knew Tieresias only as an old man, her mother told her years before Tieresias had been a female. "This prophet has experienced both sexes….maybe more," her mother had said, smiling.

"Tieresias is a venerable old gentleman," Ismene replied properly.

"And did he give you coin for passage?" Charon asked roughly.

"Yes, he said I should present it to you alone." Ismene held out the ancient money.

"Aye." Charon fingered the coins. "I suppose I am expected to endure Hades's wrath for allowing you to enter the underworld."

"I have a message for Hades that should explain…"

"Well then, you will be the recipient of Hades's wrath. Not much of an introduction to the Kingdom of Death."

Ismene heard the sound of men in the distance. "Can we begin our river crossing? I am being pursued."

Charon motioned her into the boat. Quickly, he pulled the boat away from the shore.

"Are those your pursuers?"

"Aye. Soldiers from Creon."

"Creon. I have heard of him. He has sent several people here. Not to hide, either."

Ismene thought of Creon. He was her uncle, but he did not resemble anyone in the family. His face was always pulled back almost in a sneer. When he became king after her father's departure and her mother's death, Creon had changed Thebes to a kingdom where his say was the only one. Tieresias had always been the conscience of the people, but Creon banished him to the craggy hills just beyond the city's limits. Being the youngest of Oedipus's children Ismene spent much of her youth avoiding Creon when she saw him coming down the Palace hallways. He had slapped her often, for slights he said she made, of which she was not aware; expressions on her face, not stepping to one side to let him pass...

Creon's son, Haemon, fell in love with Antigone, Ismene's older sister, and declared they would marry, over his father's objections. After that time came the short war between the two sons of Oedipus. Creon had always encouraged the rivalry between the boys, and when they both died on the battlefield, he was not unhappy.

"You are almost there," Charon said, prompting Ismene to wake from her memories. "Why would Creon seek you out?"

"He had my sister killed. And then his son who loved her followed her in death. But you know all this!"

"And only you are left. Little more than a child! What danger could you be to him?"

"Thebes loved my father, even after..."

After the truth was known that Oedipus had married his own mother and killed his father, Laius. The city mourned for Jocasta and Oedipus.

"Is it possible Creon fears the power of love over might?" Ismene put her hands to her cold cheeks and looked directly at Charon.

The ferryman's eyes were hooded, almost like a falcon, but he nodded his head, "The power of love is great, indeed. Orpheus came here for love of his new wife, Eurydice, after she died. He almost succeeded in leading her out of the Underworld."

There was a strange sound in the distance of dogs howling, one directly after the other. Ismene drew her cloak about her.

15

"Now, how do I get you past Cerberus? He knows the living from the dead. You haven't the gift of music to lull him to sleep as Orpheus did."

"Tieresias gave me a powder to throw into his many eyes…." Ismene was not looking forward to meeting this many-headed dog.

"Tieresias must love you to share his secrets with you."

"He was my father's dearest friend."

"A powerful enemy and a powerful friend. You are more interesting than you look," Charon observed. "And you will see your family once again. How will you bear it when you have to leave?"

"I will bear what I must. I have seen my father do it—the truth of his fate, blindness, madness, and finally redemption."

"And yet, you know your family is cursed through time?"

"My family is Creon's family too. That is why he fears me."

The boat bumped against the shore. Ismene turned to see torches lighting the opening of a great maw in the hillside.

"Tieresias has not given you an easy journey. I don't know if Hades, himself, is kinder than your uncle."

Charon helped her out of the boat. She swallowed her cry at the cold touch of his hand.

"I look forward to taking you to the other side when the time comes," he whispered. As she started towards the opening in the earth, he stopped her with his warning, "Hades has just lost his wife for six months. Tred softly. His temper is not the best at this time."

Ismene nodded. She knew the story of the glorious young woman who had met her mother-goddess on the other shore. Hades had fallen in love on sight with this radiant maiden and taken her to the Underworld as his queen. Demeter, the mother, had mourned so hard that the earth itself withered under her keening. Zeus had to intervene, finally, when crops died and rivers dried up. For six months, Demeter could claim her daughter, and for the other six, Perserphone was the bride of Hades. While Perserphone was reconciled with her mother, the earth blossomed. When she returned to her King of Death, the earth once more fell into a cold melancholy. And what of Perserphone? Pulled between mother and husband? Her side of the tale was never told.

"Take the pathway straight ahead. It is a rocky road. A definite step is important. Should you stumble, no one will help you rise. The dead are usually not concerned with the problems of the living…."

Ismene moved quickly into the opening, her eyes adjusting to the pathway beyond the lazing torches. The air grew colder and thinner as she descended.

She had accompanied her father through many dark woods and wild lands before he finally found peace at Colonus. Antigone was with her, but it had not kept her from terror. On that journey, she kept that terror hidden from her father who needed her guidance. Now she had herself to guide, the terror filling her throat. Again, she could hear the howling of the many-headed dog. Her hand felt the powder in a sack tied about her waist.

"You have just a few seconds of blindness when you throw this," Tieresias had said. "You must race as fast as you can into the main cave once you toss this at Cerberus."

"Will he follow me when the powder clears?" she wondered.

"No, but he will alert Hades that you are there."

"And what will Hades do? The god of death, itself!"

"Much of that depends on you, Ismene. He is not a god who is easily kind. He lives among people with violent ends, with tragic stories, with great disease. His wife barely endures him. Your skill at managing people is required. A skill you inherited from your mother and father. You are the only child who could do this."

"He sounds more like man than god."

"Hades is an unhappy god. His older brothers took the Heavens and the Earth, leaving him the kingdom no one else wanted. If you could make him smile…"

Ismene thought of what it must be like to rule over death. She wondered how a god could bear to live in such a world as the one she was approaching. Never to soar through the heavens or ride the great ocean waves. Never to walk in disguise among the humans. Never to feast with the other divinities on Olympus. He was as condemned as the humans who came here when their lives were ended. She thought of her one glimpse of his wife, Perserphone, as she had run to her mother's arms. If this maiden could not make him smile, what could Ismene do?

As her thoughts continued, so did the path, until she saw a flash of many fangs and heard a snarl before her. Sitting on a great rock ledge was Cerberus, the dog of the Underworld. Could he smell the life in her? She moved slowly, her hand taking a scoop from the powder.

The great dog was sniffing the air frantically. Then a low growl began in his many throats.

"Yes," Ismene thought. "He knows I am alien to this place."

As the great dog leaned over to sniff her, she threw the powder quickly in a half circle, blinding his many eyes.

As though she heard Tieresias's voice yell, "Now!" she took off, running past the great dog into the widening of the cave. There were several people reclining on the rocks at the edge who looked at her with some disinterest.

She kept on running. A hand reached out and stopped her, holding her by her long blonde hair.

"Enough, mistress. You have reached the land of the dead. What do you require here?" There was a metallic quality to the voice. The other hand of her captor reached around her waist, picking her up easily and carrying her through the main room. She felt the strength of her captor and did not fight him.

The powerful arms carried her along another corridor where more people stood as though at a public market. They looked with little surprise as she was taken along. Ismene tried to twist around to see who held her, but the fingers forced her head away.

"You asked what I required here," she gasped, the fingers hard on her throat. "I require audience with the mighty Hades."

The man dropped her then, with a thud, on the hard rock floor. She looked up to see her captor's angry face, his ivory-smooth skin, his disheveled black locks streaming to his shoulders, and his black robe that was askew.

"I am the mighty Hades, maiden. Who are you to come invade my kingdom? You are the second human to deceive my dog."

"I did not deceive him," she spoke primly. "I merely threw a powder in his eyes. He was obviously not deceived. You were not deceived."

"You don't have the look of the dead."

There was a pause as they regarded each other.

"Yes," she acknowledged finally, "I was not trying to deceive anyone."

He extended a hand to her. The hand that had pressed just moments before into her throat.

"Forgive me. I am in mourning. Those that are so close to the entrance are the most unhappy....we mourn for the living."

His wife! He was mourning for Perserphone! Of course!

"I understand the mighty Hades's loss." She took his hand and let him pull her to her feet. He towered over her by almost a foot.

"You are not the person I wanted to come by the great dog," he muttered.

Make him smile, Ismene. How?

His black eyes were ringed in the red that distinguished weeping. Nevertheless, she would try.

"Tieresias sent me to you," she said.

The name of the prophet had made Charon smile. It had the opposite effect on Hades. He frowned.

"I don't want the troubles of that old man. He will come here himself soon enough, to stir up mischief for eternity."

"He said you would hide me." This was not exactly true. What Tieresias had said was that Ismene *should* hide there, not that Hades *would* hide her.

"From whom are you hiding?"

"My uncle's troops."

"Why did he not send you to Olympus? He's on much better terms with my brother, Zeus."

"I don't know….. perhaps Zeus is not as kind…."

Wrong word! Hades spat in contempt.

"Maybe he thought a living maiden would be of some solace in the months you must pass until the return of your wife from her mother's home," Ismene said this all in one breath. "His message was for you to be patient with me."

"What? You would replace my wife?" Hades was indignant.

"Only a shadow of her. But, I can tell you the gossip of the world....I did not mean...," she left that thought unfinished. Ismene pulled her robes tighter around her.

Whatever he thought she meant, Hades's eyes filled up with tears. He was far from smiling.

"And who is this maiden who thinks she can be a companion to the Lord of Death?"

"I am Ismene, daughter of Oedipus and Jocasta, rulers of Thebes."

"Your family is all here, except yourself. Well, now you are here, too. Only in passing. What keeps me from flinging you back into the world?"

She swallowed hard, "Loneliness."

"In the name of all…" He hand pulled her along after him down the hallway to a chamber. He harshly pushed her down onto a couch.

"You are a presumptuous child. Why do you think you can say such things to me?" he thundered.

"I have nothing to lose, mighty Hades. If you fling me out , I will be killed. Then you will be stuck with me for all eternity."

Then it came, that smile, like the sun through the angriest of storm clouds.

"You should be whipped," he said.

"I would rather be fed," she countered.

"Now I must feed you as well?"

"If you want me to go on living…"

"I will keep you alive in the land of the dead. That is what Tieresias is asking of me?"

"Yes."

"Ah, well.." Hades shrugged. "How long must you stay?"

"Tieresias will send for me."

"I hope he does not come, himself. I am still angry with him for…," Hades stopped. "But that is not your concern. Food is your concern. Warmth is your concern. I know these concerns, because my wife has the same. She, too, is a living woman. The others here are but shadows. Your family, too. They have wasted into the bare outlines of themselves. Death diminishes."

He smiled again, more easily this time.

"They told me you had a very bad temper," Ismene smiled back.

"I do."

She looked around the room which seemed to sparkle from every wall.

"Is this where I am to stay?"

"No, foolish girl. This is my room. Yours will be with your family."

A longing rose in her for the old days with her family when she was young and curled into her mother's lap.

"But I may come and visit with you?"

He shook out his long locks. "Not unless I send for you. Remember that I am in mourning."

"It is not correct to mourn for someone still alive."

"You are not to remind me of what I can do. I am a god, and you are a very young, very weak little girl."

"But you must mourn every year this way...."

"Yes, and I have Tieresias to thank. He was the one who pleaded my case to my brother, Zeus. Pleaded badly."

"Pleaded well. You have her half the year, after carrying her off against her will. That was generous of Zeus."

"I say again, you should be whipped. This time I am not smiling."

She saw his immense muscles tensing against his robes. His eyes were deeper black than the night without a moon.

"I hope not to displease you, Hades."

"Then I will take you to your family. You will let me weep this night for the bride I chose that day, who is now denied me...."

* * *

Hades guided her along the hallway from his chamber to a lake. Around the lake, people moved slowly. Ismene observed they were dressed in gray and made no eye contact. At first, they did not acknowledge Hades's presence, but then she saw their hands go to their foreheads in some slight salute to the god.

"It's so quiet," she breathed. "As quiet as a grave."

"Yes. It is a grave. Remember?" Hades did not look back as he spoke.

"Is it always this silent?"

"We have some musicians who play once in a while. The dead have little to say."

"Is this what you prefer?"

"No. I prefer the voice of my wife, the lute of Orpheus, the singing of birds. My brothers set me here without asking my preference because I was the youngest."

"I did not realize even gods don't always get what they wish for."

He was compelled to turn then, "You are a most insightful maiden. It will do no harm to cultivate that element of you. In the world, you will need such a skill."

She suddenly liked him. His disarray and his anger cloaked the handsome figure beneath. Tieresias's message was for Hades to be patient. With her? himself?

"I hope you send for me, Hades. I would like to talk with you when…"

"I mourn until my wife's return, Ismene."

"But wouldn't she want you to be happier than you appear now? She must be happy at home with her mother."

"She doesn't think of me at all when she is on the earth. I am cursed with a woman who does not love me."

"You can earn love, Hades."

"I am a rapist." He shut his eyes against the words. "I took her against her will."

"And yet you mourn her when she is absent. That sounds more like a man in love."

They were walking during the course of the conversation around the lake to an aperture.

"Your family is within," he bowed slightly. "I leave you to make your own explanations for being in this odd situation."

"Please, send for me…." She put her hand on his great arm. He recoiled.

"Perhaps." Again, he bowed and strode away. She watched his departure with an odd chill.

There was a white light shining from the aperture. As she entered, Ismene saw her family grouped as she had remembered them. In addition, Haemon was there, his arm about Antigone's shoulder. They all looked up at once.

"I thought we should never meet again," Ismene sighed.

"Then you did not listen to the myths I told you about this place." Her mother came forward, embracing her youngest daughter. The embrace was colder than ice. Ismene tried not to pull back.

"Are you one of us?" Oedipus asked. His eyes were restored in death.

"No. I am here for a short time only. Hiding." She looked reluctantly towards Haemon. "Hiding from Creon's soldiers."

"And what have you done to anger him?" Antigone spoke with some scorn. Ismene had refused to help bury her brother, against Creon's orders. Antigone had taken on the task alone.

"I have lived, sister, which he believes is as much a crime against the state as dying."

"How is it you can hide here?"

"Tieresias sent me...."

"He was right to do so." Oedipus took her in his arms. Again, she felt the chill. "Tieresias knows that Creon can be unrelenting."

Ismene looked at them in disbelief. "I am cold. I am very hungry."

"We have no food. We need none. We are dead," Antigone said, her voice somewhat gentler.

"Then, what am I to do? Hades said he would feed me and keep me warm, but he is distracted...."

"You have met Hades?" Oedipus was incredulous.

"Yes, father. He carried me to his chamber, dumped me on the floor and threatened to whip me. I doubt he has given me another thought after bringing me here...."

At that moment, the form of a young girl appeared, carrying a wine flask and some bread. Over her arm was a cloak.

"For the living...," was all the young girl said, depositing the items on a rock ledge.

"You have made a friend of Hades," her mother said with some awe.

"I made him smile." Ismene put the cloak around her and began to eat the bread.

"Smile? The King of Death?" Antigone moved to Ismene's side.

"Is it so rare that he smiles?"

"Only when his wife is in residence."

Ismene was smiling, herself, the wine warming her. "He should smile all the time. This is a gloomy place."

"It is the Underworld...."

"Still, it need not be gloomy. Why should eternity be gloomy?"

"You do not understand. Hades has six moons of joy. These are not those moons."

Ismene wiped the wine from her lips. "Yes, mother, I know the story. He told me he mourns until her return."

"And then he torments the poor woman with questions about what she did in those lost moons, whom she saw, where she walked...," Antigone explained.

"Be quiet, daughter! Hades has ears everywhere!" Oedipus admonished his older child.

"What more can he do to us? We are already dead," Haemon shrugged.

"Are you so frightened of him?" Ismene wondered.

"As fearful of him as you are of Creon," Jocasta said.

"Hades tried to make me fear him, but Tieresias knew I could get him to smile...," Ismene chewed the bread. She was feeling much improved, and the god had not forgotten her when he left her with her family.

"But you must be weary." Her mother ran a frosty hand over Ismene's forehead. "I will show you a darker chamber where you might sleep."

"Do you not sleep?"

"What use would we have for sleep? Sleep is for the living, to sort out their dreams. Our dreams are over," Haemon spoke.

"Then let me sleep and remember I am still alive," Ismene nodded her head. Her sleep came quickly. The robe Hades had sent her kept her warm and secure.

* * *

When Ismene awoke, the dark chamber was sparkling much like Hades's room. She sat up abruptly. The young girl who had brought the food before was shining the walls with a cloth.

"There is water to wash. Bread and wine are by the doorway," the young girl said.

"And who are you?"

"I am naught but a shade," the girl said. She stood back to admire the sparkle of cave crystals. "I am an emanation of Lord Hades's mind. You can call me Umbra if you must name me."

"And where is my family?" Ismene peered into the main chamber.

Umbra turned her almost transparent form to face Ismene, "They are about their day. No one is idle in death."

"I do not understand what one does for eternity."

"Many things. Depending on how one lived. Some just suffer as they made others do. You have heard their legends...."

"Yes, I have heard the tales of eternal misery."

"Others spend their time improving the lives of those still above the earth."

Ismene poured herself the watered wine. "Can this world reach into the world where I exist?"

"Oh yes, maiden. No world is exclusive. Poseidon often neglects his oceans in order to come visit his youngest brother here. Lord Hades, as well, has been invited to Olympus, although not since Zeus decided in favor of Demeter's claim that she should share her daughter with our king."

"And what is my task here?" Ismene wondered.

"Lord Hades is puzzled as to your task. He found you a great surprise."

"He must find me a task , if I am to stay here. At home, I had my lessons. Here, I will go mad without some occupation."

"It is scarcely Hades's place to find amusement for someone who has intruded so rudely on his world." Umbra's sharp tone surprised Ismene. She was not used to servants speaking so bluntly. She had to remind herself Umbra was not really a servant, but rather some shadow animated by the will of Hades. It was Hades's words in the mouth of something less than a ghost.

"Go tell Lord Hades that Tieresias expects me to be treated with the utmost kindness. This is not utmost kindness."

"You will tell Lord Hades such things yourself!" Umbra turned on her heel. "My advice, if you will listen, is not to tell Lord Hades anything unpleasant."

So saying, Umbra left Ismene alone in the shining cave. Two days ago, Ismene had sat in the castle courtyard at Thebes singing with her friends about the legend of Perserphone. Now, she was here in the land of death, subject to the whims of a mourning god. She had just called his behavior unacceptable. It was this very quality of speaking her mind that had angered Creon to the point of seeking her life.

"I will try to guard my tongue," she vowed.

With a quick movement, she went to the cave entrance and retrieved the bread and wine. After eating, she washed in the basin of cold water, readjusting her blue robes and plaiting her long blonde hair. Stepping from the inner chamber, she looked at the underground lake where Hades had led her the previous night. Although there were no trees or guideposts to remind her of the upper world, the lake seemed familiar. The waters lapped calmly against the brown rocks like an animal drinking up the silence. Briefly she tried to remember from which direction Hades had brought her. She had a quick desire to seek him out. Then, she thought better of it. It was not only her tongue that often landed her in trouble, but her impulses as well. What had she to say to a god? Gods were better addressed through priests and oracles. Yes, and prophets such as Tieresias.

Her father had taken her to Delphi with him once. It was a journey he had not wished to make. He had almost sent Tieresias instead. He took her only because she cried so pitifully. Antigone rarely cried. Antigone was too proud for tears. Ismene learned early that weeping was the prompt that could bring her parents to her will. Her nurse was not as pliable.

The long chariot ride that spread over many days and landscapes before reaching Delphi afforded her father time to tell her his adventures. He told her of the strange prophecy the oracle gave him many years ago that he would wed his mother and kill his father. Ismene puzzled over the possibility that the oracle was a fake. Oedipus, after all, had been adopted as a baby. He was found by a shepherd, a child exposed. Such children were usually left. Fate was not to be contradicted. This shepherd, however, took the infant with the loud lungs for weeping to the king and queen of the land. They raised him as their own child. It was only after he found out years later of his adoption that he went to Delphi to learn of his origins. The oracle did not tell him his biography. Instead, she couched her words into one piece of advice, "Flee, Oedipus, before your hand causes more pain."

And so he had fled the land he had known, the parents he believed were his biological creators, and had gone as far as he could go to avoid causing pain. And almost the first thing he did was to kill his actual father in a quarrel over who should step aside on meeting in a narrow passage of a road. After that, he committed his second sin by winning the hand of the dead man's queen, his mother. At the time of their journey to Delphi, Oedipus was unaware of the second part of the story. He had looked towards the visit to the oracle with hope. His kingdom had been afflicted with a plague. He had sought the advice of the Oracle to end the suffering of his subjects.

Ismene, who had rarely been out of the palace grounds, took the ride as her first adventure. She had looked in wonder at the rugged landscapes that passed by. Her father was almost giddy with joy by the time they arrived in Delphi. It was sunset. The sky bled red over the face of that day. Ismene had walked with her father to the edge of the cave where the Oracle dwelled. The smell of sulfur had filled her nostrils. She had drawn back even as her father urged her not to be afraid.

"You must stand here alone while I speak with the Oracle. Then we will find lodgings for the night....stand here with the horses. Calm them. You have a way with creatures," he urged.

He paused several minutes before actually entering the cave. The horses pawed the earth, anxious to be off. Ismene, thankful for some task, found some sweet grasses for them to eat from her hands. After that, the two horses were still. Ismene sat on the ground next to them, watching the stars blink into her evening sight. She was unaware of the passage of time, but at one point a great cry came from the cave, a cry so loud it might have been made by a city of people rather than one man. The horses reared up. It was then, Ismene wished her father had taken Tieresias's offer to accompany him.

"A man never knows the language of such an oracle unless he has first spoken with Hades," Tieresias had warned. "This oracle speaks with a voice that goes beyond our world. Our world is safe in words....her words present danger."

Oedipus laughed, "You are over-stressing your importance as usual, prophet. Go back to your bones and entrails....I have visited this oracle before."

Tieresias went off, shaking his head, leaning on his stick with just a touch more heaviness. Ismene ran after the old figure.

"Will I ever speak with Hades?" she asked, tugging at the arm of the prophet.

"Yes, Ismene, and more will you do with Hades. You will surprise even the oracle," Tieresias laughed, shaking her hand away.

As Ismene stood before the oracle's cave, she remembered Tieresias's words. She wondered about this oracle who could speak the truth and deceive both at the same time. Curiously she crept closer to the cave's entrance. Her father was on his knees before a large fire in which burned the face of a wizened woman, the flame crackling about those features but never consuming the image.

"You cannot beg to change the truth," the woman's face curled in scorn. "Your fate is already woven into the tapestry. The thread will be cut away."

"And my city? My people?"

"They will curse you, but they will honor your daughters."

"Not my sons?"

"Your sons will battle over your name like two spoiled children over a toy. Your daughters will redeem that name...."

Ismene saw her father's back curl over until his forehead was touching the ground, "I must know how to save my city..."

"You already know, Oedipus. You knew before you came here. You knew last night when you lay beside your wife in your royal bed. The two of you must acknowledge your crime…."

"How was it a crime to love?"

"Need I name your crime again?" The voice bellowed. "And before your daughter who is watching us?"

Oedipus turned in horror. Ismene came to him and took his hand. "Let us go, father. This oracle is done."

Her father pulled his hand away. "I am not done…."

"Oh, yes, Oedipus. This daughter is correct. You must leave now….or hear in plain words what you cannot even bear veiled."

And so he sped up the ledge and out into the night, Ismene following on his heels. She made a sign to the horses who pawed the ground. They raised their heads to smell the fear.

"Father, please," she begged, coming upon him. vomiting at the edge of a small lake. "Father, you must rest!"

"My whole life has been a sleeping. Now is the time to rise up." He turned to her, his eyes blazing with the same energies as the horses.

"Father, the horses are tired. I am tired," she protested.

"Then sleep. I will walk on ahead. When you are refreshed, follow the road. You will find me."

He began to stride purposefully forward. She went back to the horses, untying them from the chariot. Gathering their muzzles in her hands she whispered to them, "We must protect each other."

When she awoke, the horses were calmly grazing. The cave had no odors rising from it. The larks danced above her head. It was daytime, a world she felt comfortable in. Quickly she walked to the cave and looked within. There was no fire, no face. Only a cave, cool and distant from the bake of day.

Ismene knew how to drive the chariot. She let the horses find their own clip along the dirt road. Finally, she saw her father, still walking in his purposeful stride. He smiled as the chariot approached. She smiled back as he came nearer. It was as though the oracle had never spoken.

In Thebes, Oedipus went quickly into the palace ignoring the crowds of stricken citizens who camped out on the steps. Ismene touched one or two of them, but she had to hurry on to keep pace with her father. Tieresias was in the throne room, talking to Jocasta.

"I found my answer, old man," Oedipus said simply.

"I can see that," replied the blind prophet. His trembling hand reached out to explore Oedipus's face. "And do you believe this answer?"

"I need proof," Oedipus murmured. "It is not an answer easy to believe without proof."

"Husband, you asked her a simple question—who murdered Laius?—whoever murdered my first husband cursed our city. She must have given you a simple answer." Jocasta shivered the length of her body. Ismene was drawn in by a maternal arm and hid her face in her mother's bosom. The smell of her mother calmed her.

"Send the child away," Tieresias urged. "She is too young...."

"I saw the oracle's face," Ismene said proudly. "I saw her face and heard her voice."

Jocasta spun around to Oedipus, "You promised you would not take her in to that den....to that mother of wolves."

"I did not take her. You know Ismene will never do what she is asked if her curiosity is contrary to the request. She followed me inside."

"How much did she hear?" Tieresias's voice now expressed concern.

"Nothing! Less than nothing!" Oedipus looked beseechingly at Ismene.

"I heard her say Antigone and I would bring honor back to our name," Ismene spoke in a small voice.

"The House of Atreus, forever cursed. Did the oracle mean your children could break the curse?" Tieresias asked.

"She did not explain. Does she ever explain? It is all a riddle to which Time finds answers," Oedipus exclaimed. He was gently untangling Ismene from her mother's garments. "Child, you must go find your nurse now.."

His voice had an edge to it that Ismene knew meant no tears would dissuade him from sending her away.

"Yes, father." Ismene ran quickly from the room. Her heart was pounding. She looked for her nurse in the bedchamber and then ran into the garden where Antigone was sitting, her hands to her cheeks.

"You're back," Antigone observed without moving. She was several years older than Ismene. Her dark eyes were half-closed against the glare of the sunshine.

"You should have come with us," Ismene said, hoping her sister might ask more.

"I wanted to go to the festival. Even with all the tragedies they held the festival....and I kissed Haemon."

"Did he kiss you back?"

Antigone 's mouth widened into a smile, "He kissed back, sister. It was more exciting than a visit to the Oracle."

Ismene tried to picture Antigone and Haemon kissing. Her sister was almost as tall as Haemon. Both were considered very beautiful to behold. Was it the way Oedipus and Jocasta kissed when they thought no one was watching them?

"You must marry him if you kissed him," Ismene spoke in a prim little voice.

"We will marry. Haemon will come to Father soon."

"I am happy for you." Ismene loved her sister in the way a only a child can adore beauty. Impulsively she threw her arms around Antigone, pressing her tight.

"Someday you, too, will kiss a boy the way I kissed Haemon." Antigone accepted the embrace without returning it.

This morning in the underworld Ismene, thought on those words. Here she was in the land of death without ever having that promised kiss. She hoped Tieresias would not forget her here. As though Tieresias forgot anything! He was always reminding her of moments of her own life that she, herself, had forgotten.

Ismene was sitting on a ledge overlooking the great lake before the chambers where Hades had brought her to find her family the night before. A hand slipped around her waist. With a small cry of surprise, she turned to find Antigone.

"I was thinking of you," Ismene said. "Of the day you told me Haemon kissed you."

31

"The day our father found out the truth. Much more important than the kiss of a maiden," Antigone's voice dripped sadness.

"Oh, that dark truth that cancelled out all the pleasures we should know!" Ismene cried.

"It changed my wedding day to the promise of a funeral."

"And put us under Creon's thumb...," Ismene scowled. "Creon, who proved no friend to those who had befriended him. Even our brother, Eteocles, who defended him against our other brother, Polyneices."

"Tell me, has Creon not grown soft over so many years?"

"Creon is crueler every day. He blames father for all his misfortunes."

"And you, my little sister. I think he bears no love for you."

"No love at all."

Ismene's blue eyes filled with tears. She was determined not to cry. Now she was a grown woman who did not throw tantrums to elicit sympathy or get her way.

"I am sorry you have had to live all these years since my death without love," Antigone touched her sister's cheek.

"Not without love. Tieresias loves me. He always let me visit him in his eyrie after Creon banished him from the city. There I could say anything I liked, and Tieresias always understood...."

"But there are other loves a young woman needs more."

"Creon would not let a man near me. He watched over me with the vigilance of a hawk. He said no further of our father's family should survive."

"And now, again, you are separated from men. Living men. Tieresias protects you from that love as well. I always thought him a jealous old man." Antigone gave a bitter smile.

"No, sister. You have never understood Tieresias," Ismene protested.

"I never understood you or that old bird on the hill," Antigone laughed. "Tieresias never had time for me."

"You were mother's daughter. He never approved of mother."

"Because she married after the death of her first husband? It was her duty as queen, although I believe she loves our father. Well then, maybe he approved too much of mother. Maybe he was jealous she married at all….to anyone but him. You have yet to discover passion, my sister. It is a powerful poison." Her eyes narrowed. "So, you think I am mother's daughter, and you are father's? Who stood up for the brother Creon did not love? I did. And lost my life while you kept yours. You would not cross Creon."

"I was young. Creon had not shown me the face behind his smiling mask. Do not blame me through eternity…." Ismene fought the tears that rose quickly. "You were right that day, and I was wrong. The oracle said we would both redeem our father's name. Perhaps I was meant to fight for it now…."

"Of what use can you be here where all deeds have been done and reckoned?"

Antigone's dark eyes blazed, fires at midnight. She was her most beautiful in these moments of anger. Ismene remembered how Antigone used to pick fights with Haemon when they were children so that he could admire her terrible rage.

"I am not of use yet, sister, but Tieresias only hides me here to summon me when I am needed."

"Then he should summon you soon. Creon is amassing an army to attack the kingdom of Corinth.. The kingdom that sheltered Polynieces. He has waited years for this opportunity. It would mean death and destruction to all who hold freedom dear."

"How do you know this?" Ismene whispered.

"We have a cave with walls as smooth as mirrors, on which we see the world as it is today…. Hades lets us look and suggest solutions to the problems we see there."

"You are spies for the god of death?"

"We are spies for no one. We do not have to look. Nor suggest."

"Take me to this cave!" Ismene pulled on Antigone's arm.

"Only Hades can give permission for you….you are not one of us." Antigone shook her head.

"Then take me to Hades…."

She remembered Hades's temper and the strength of his arms as he had carried her into his chambers. Fear raced through her. Last night, he seemed approachable, but after a night's sleep, only his rage and power remained in her mind.

"You must find Hades for yourself. I have other tasks today," Antigone sighed. "There are souls in torment that I console....souls who never will know peace. Not in any world."

So saying, the slender form of Antigone moved quickly away, leaving Ismene once more alone by the great lake. Ismene tried to remember how life had been before the dreaded words of the oracle, when her mother and father were happy together in Thebes. Her nurse had been picked from the childless women of the town with great care. The brothers were each other's most intense rival. But Ismene and Antigone, raised by this loving nurse, had days of sheer joy until the plague struck the city. Until the prophet came to the palace to demand Oedipus solve the increasingly bad conditions of his subjects. Tieresias was all-fire that day, storming up and down before her father. Oedipus sat on the throne looking like a scolded schoolboy. Jocasta alone shouted back that catastrophes were not always brought on by the wrath of the gods, sometimes just by ill luck. Tieresias stood his ground. Oedipus went with Ismene to Delphi, and the world changed forever.

"How do I alert the Corinthians from here in the land of death?" Ismene wondered. "Why did Tieresias send me here? I could have gone to Corinth, offered myself as an exile, and advised them as to Creon's character."

"You could have done so. But you listened to that senile old man," a voice boomed behind her. She knew the voice, heavy with displeasure.

"Hades," she breathed out the name.

He turned her with his hand. She looked into the midnight of his eyes.

"Do you read my thoughts now, Hades?"

"I can read thoughts," his voice was suddenly light.

"Then you know how serious..."

His frown made her stop mid-sentence.

"Things of life are transitory. You learn that lesson only in death....or where death dwells. Does it matter so much who rules Thebes or Corinth?"

"If you have looked in the mirror cave, then you have seen Creon move like a spider year after year until his web is far flung," she countered.

"I do not look in the mirror cave. The life of the living does not interest me. It only interests those who have lived...."

"Not just a peek to see what Perserphone is doing?" she teased. His hand came up to strike her, then fell.

"Everyone thinks my marriage a great comedy!" he said.

"Or a great tragedy..." Her voice softened.

She noticed his hair, so wild yesterday, was oiled and pulled back. His robes were clean. He resembled the ruler god he was.

"Is there no way I can communicate with Tieresias? To warn him? To have him warn the Corinthians?"

"I cannot allow you to communicate with that old troublemaker, but I can alert my brother, Zeus. He is committed to a time of peace. Since the great war of Troy, he has tired to earthly squabbles."

"As have most men, excepting my uncle. Perhaps because it is this Age when musicians and poets thrive. Creon says such pursuits were not manly. He may feel the virility go out of his warriors. He is a great believer in the phallic principle."

Hades frowned. "Such words from a maiden!"

"My life has been such that I have seen more than many a crone," Ismene retorted.

"I would not brag of it. It does not add to your attractiveness," Hades said. "Bragging is something spoiled young boys indulge in."

"It is no brag. I wish my life had been otherwise. My family is cursed. Did you know?"

"Yes, I have had every one of them here, except you and your uncle, Creon. And now you. But not for long. You are even more eager than my wife to return to the earth above."

The earth above! She had been here in the nether regions no more than a day, but already she longed for the clear push of the wind, the heady smell of the meadow near Tieresias's eyrie, and the deep suck of daylight. How did Perserphone return here again and again after six months of life's beauties! Even to a god who loved her!

Hades gave an impatient grunt as though her thoughts were known.

"You will not want my uncle once he is here. He would try to take away authority even from you, Hades. Even from a god."

"You think I have not been challenged before? No sooner did the warriors descend from Troy's great war than did they decide to fight me. I could not kill them! They were already dead. But I meted out punishment, against the wishes of the other gods who had championed them."

She sat on the ledge as he talked and moved in an angry circle. "Even Hector? Even Achilles? Ajax?"

He nodded at the sounds of their names.

"You know these men. They were like your brothers....arrogant, because they had shields and swords. Because that fool Homer took it into his head to sing their stories everywhere. Celebrity is a drug like no other."

It struck her how alone he was. On Olympus, the gods co-mingled, sharing their virtues and vices. Here Hades had no one to share with that was of his stature. He could not ask for counsel. She hoped he was trying to be a wise king. Her father had tried and failed to provide wisdom, except at Colonus, when it mattered only to him.

"Homer had tried to sing his songs to a village that sprung up near the ruins of Troy. They stoned him to death, the villagers did...," she said aloud.

"Now he wanders my kingdom, blasting our ears with that much-embellished battle," Hades laughed. She laughed with him. It was good to laugh suddenly, spontaneously, even in the bowels of death.

From the corner of her eye, she saw her mother and father standing at a distance, their faces registering the shock of seeing their youngest child laughing with the god of death. Quickly she leapt to her feet, smoothing down her laughter into a serious expression.

As Hades turned to acknowledge her parents, they bowed low to him. In their lives, they had others bow the same way to them. They had been king and queen of a great kingdom.

"Forgive us, Lord of Death," Oedipus spoke in formal voice. "We were seeking our daughter for news...."

"Of your former world?" Hades finished the thought for Oedipus. "Yes, she is filled with chatter. I am done speaking with her." With that, he strode away.

"You were laughing together, and yet he sounded displeased with you." Her mother hurried to her side.

"His anger is like a summer storm that blows away quickly, I think," Ismene smiled at the retreating figure of the god. "In any event, he has little patience with talk of the world above his head."

She drew her parents in, linking arms with them both.

"Tell us what has happened," her father urged.

"Creon kept me prisoner in his palace after Antigone died….and Haemon. Then he banished Tieresias from the city. I now understand why he suddenly decided to have me taken into deeper captivity. Antigone told me he plans to mount an attack on Corinth. After all these years. He has been planning for some time, I think. I remember midnight meetings with his generals. But I escaped. A slave at the palace told me of something he had overheard. Tieresias sheltered me for the night, but in the morning, he bade me hide here where Creon would not think to look. I do not know if Creon's men followed me to Tieresias's eyrie."

"Tieresias is a wise man," her mother sighed.

"You did not always think so," Ismene reminded her sharply.

"Oh, yes, my daughter. That is why I feared him. Because of his wisdom. With Creon, it is the opposite. I fear his stupidity. When Laius was alive…," Jocasta stopped, looking to Oedipus.

"Speak of it, Jocasta. I cannot fault you for remembering your other husband…."

"And your father," Jocasta reminded him.

"I did not know him as such. To me, he was a man who stood in my way when I was impatient."

"Laius always trusted Tieresias. Our kingdom was a prosperous one. My only sorrow was the death of my child. Or so I thought."

Ismene watched the play of emotions on her mother's face. Although Jocasta was older by fifteen years than Oedipus, her face retained a youthful beauty. It was odd that Antigone was favored by her mother, when Ismene was the daughter who most resembled Jocasta. Maybe it was their tempers which could match each other when aroused. Ismene, like her father, was slow to anger. Oedipus had a bad temper which he kept watch over since killing the man at the crossroads. The man who turned out to be his own father.

"You should have killed me, yourself, when I was an infant." Oedipus shook his head, remembering how he had been raised as a prince in another kingdom.

"I did not have the heart. A mother's love…," Jocasta sighed, and suddenly she flung herself into Oedipus's arms. He held her close, making soothing sounds he used to calm Ismene when she was frightened as a child.

"Do you ever see Laius, mother? Surely, he resides in this great nether world as well."

Jocasta looked in surprise at her daughter, "Yes, I have seen him at a great distance. There are many warriors here that dwell together. It is there that I see Laius. I do not seek him out."

"And do you want to speak with him, father?"

"Why should I speak with him? I am known to him only as the man who slew him."

Ismene knew there were currents that ran between her parents that she did not understand. Perhaps Antigone knew better how to comfort them in their strange love, since Antigone had experienced that love between adults.

Tieresias had smiled when she once asked him about such love. "There are those who will give you simple answers, but the question is very complicated. I have been fortunate, Ismene, for I have known such feelings as both male and female…." Then he gave a small laugh. "I see the surprise of your face. Yes, once I was female. My blood flowed from between my legs once a month just as yours does. But then I did not have this gift of foresight. I was confused by the urgings of my heart. And I fell in love. Fell, yes. That is the correct term. I fell in love. The man was a great warrior. He took me into his household over the objections of his wife. He took me into his bed, too. Do you know what that means?"

"Of course," she said, her voice no louder than a whisper. Her nurse had explained it to her one day when two horses were mating in the fields. "I know it happens wherever animals, men, and gods exist....and sometimes between animals, men, and gods."

"Your nurse explained it badly," Tieresias snapped. "She is one of those who does not understand how deep an experience it can be. It can topple kingdoms....it did for your parents."

He was quiet for a moment, expecting her to respond, but she stood still against the rocks, waiting for him to continue.

"This general loved me. He showed me that in loving me he could give me such pleasures...." Again Tieresias was still. "And to receive these pleasures, I learned to create joys for him."

"And how did it end?"

"His wife complained to Zeus."

Complained to a god? About the simple matter of a man and his servant? "This woman must have had great power to reach Zeus's ears...."

"If only it had reached Zeus's ears. The ears that listened to the complaint were Hera's, Zeus's much-betrayed wife, who sympathized with the woman...."

There was a statue of Hera in Thebes. The face was serious and a little sad. Not a young goddess. A goddess who had known the flaws of her mighty husband.

"She did not wait to ask Zeus about how to proceed. She went into his thoughts as he slept and extracted the means to her revenge....on men. And on myself."

"Which was?"

"She turned me into a man. Took away my beautiful breasts, my slender waist, my glorious crypt of treasures....Zeus was furious with her, but he would not change me back. To apologize for his wife's rage, he gave me the gift of prophecy, binding me to a world beyond that of the flesh. I tasted the appetites of the body afterwards, but it was never the same. Never was a woman as good to love...."

"You miss your womanhood?"

"More than you will ever know," Tieresias sighed. "We are but a moment of light. Then forever, we keep Hades company. I would like the ecstasy of my light burning hot. I keep a cool flame now."

"I do not understand this need of men for women."

"It will happen so soon, Ismene, you will think you have blinked between the time I tell you and the moment you feel it, too, but like with me, your romantic life will give way to another existence."

"I will not be a mother?"

"Nor a father. Do not look so surprised. Your life will be envied by many who hear it sung in the next ages."

She had turned away, disturbed by his words. She did not want to be sung about! Her family had already been immortalized through a curse long before her birth. She wanted another kind of life. The simple one she saw every day as she looked from the palace to where children laughed, mothers scolded, and young lovers pushed each other into the heat of the city wall.

Now she saw her parents again after their destinies had been unrolled and deciphered. They were still in love, but they were unhappy even in death. Antigone and Haemon, as well, clung to each other with a kind of desperation that might have become so much else if not cursed by Atreus and his actions.

"Child...," her father came to her, breaking her reverie, "we are not able to help you now."

"Yes, father, I know." She attempted a smile. "It is no matter. I must help myself. I think that is why Tieresias would not keep me with him. He knows he, too, must pass to this place, while I must continue my life. I must find my own way to deal with Creon...."

"And there is no man who might protect you?" Her mother strode over to Ismene. "It is unthinkable that Creon did not find you a protector."

"But, mother, he never meant to protect me. Or Antigone."

"He promised your father there at the end...," Jocasta's voice trailed off.

"He let us live. That was his first mistake in his own eyes. Antigone grew up to challenge him. And Haemon followed her."

Ismene took Jocasta's cold hand. For the first time, Ismene accepted that her destiny was not the one she desired. She had to come to the land of death to accept the terms of her life. It was possible to think of Tieresias smiling far-off in his eyrie at this moment.

"What do I do in this place?" she wondered aloud.

"What most of us did on the earth above. Live. You are still of flesh and blood," her father said. "This place must be something better than the prison where Creon meant to keep you. Learn while you are here. There are many among us who might give you wisdom."

Ismene looked into her father's restored eyes, those eyes that always had a slow burn of passion behind each word. When he lost his eyes, she had looked for that burn again in his voice, his walk. Only at the end in Colonus, under that small olive tree, before his death, did she hear something that matched the burn. His death was so simple that she and Antigone were not aware of the moment. They were looking at the great sky above, thinking only of the sudden peace after the wind died down. What frightened Ismene most about her father's death was that the moment seemed so inconsequential, braided into other moments.

"Oh father, I need your wisdom," Ismene grabbed Oedipus's chilly hand. "I know you learned from your blindness....just as Tieresias learns from his."

"I do not think there are words for the wisdom I gathered before my death. Such knowledge is beyond words. And of no importance here."

She thought of Hades's eyes that were the deepest black she had ever seen. The Lord of Death whose eyes admitted no light. What knowledge did he possess?

"I cannot believe we live all our lives only to learn so that we might spend the time afterwards denying that knowledge."

"Believe it, my daughter. When Tieresias releases you from this place, do not seek to return until you are old, beyond help," Jocasta warned.

Ismene held her two parents until the chill of their substance was numbing her. Then she released them.

"I will walk…seek out those you say can help me, father," Ismene said at last. She wished to be gone from them.

Her footsteps took her further into the earth, a long path of hard stones that cut her feet in spite of the sandals she wore. Ahead, she saw Haemon moving. She called out to him, and he stopped, guiltily.

"Where are you going?" Ismene ran to catch up with him.

"Sometimes, I go to see others." Haemon looked at her with unease. "You will not tell them you saw me…."

"Oh, Haemon, I was always shadowing you as a child. I never told some of the places you went." Ismene laughed. Haemon blushed. Once she had followed him to the house of a famous courtesan. He had been very angry with her when he saw her ducking behind a pillar. The courtesan, Elena, had laughed, telling Haemon Ismene did not even understand what a courtesan was. Haemon retorted that meant Ismene would ask Antigone.

"You did not want Antigone to know where you had been. I blackmailed you for weeks with that one," Ismene smiled.

"Until your nurse found out….overhearing you bragging to me about how you could follow me anywhere," Haemon smiled back.

"Yes, then I was punished. And Antigone was angry with you for six whole months," Ismene finished the story. By this time, she was striding at his side. "Where are you going now, Haemon?" Her voice was softer.

"To see my mother."

"And why is that such a secret?"

"She is Creon's wife."

"I always liked your mother."

"Antigone did not like her. My mother told Antigone how spoiled your brothers were…."

"And they were spoiled. My father and mother doted on them."

"Tell me, did my father remarry?" Haemon put an anxious hand on Ismene's arm.

"No. He truly mourned your mother. He mourned you, too. But he was hard on the rest of us. Tieresias could not come to the city. I was badly treated."

"I do not regret my decision," Haemon looked straight ahead.

"But I believe he regretted his. In the darkest part of the night, I have heard him cry out the way my father cried at the oracle's."

"My mother cries, too. She sits in the darkest part of this land of death and wails. She could not believe my father was that unjust. She knew him as a private man. To her, he was everything until that day...," Haemon's voice trailed off.

Ismene walked beside him, unable to speak. She thought of that time when Eurydice ran from the throne room, after hearing that Haemon was dead, Antigone was walled up, suffocating, as Creon told his wife the sentence. The poison was a quick gesture for so long a marriage. The two had been no more than children when they met, much like Haemon and Antigone. Despite a slight limp, which came from one shortened leg, Eurydice was admired by men and women alike for her elegance. Jocasta always consulted her for attire, child-rearing advice, the best wine to serve at banquets. Only Haemon's death could have driven this woman from the sight of her husband to the poisoned chalice.

"I...loved your mother," Ismene breathed at last.

"Yes, she knew that. She loved you, too. She told me you were often the child last to know...."

"Know what?"

"The other three—even my beloved Antigone—fought for attention. You were happy with so little compared to your siblings. Eurydice admired that in you....that you were not greedy. She did not admire Antigone, except her beauty."

"No mother, I believe, admires her son's lover."

Haemon turned, cupped Ismene's chin with his hand, and laughed, "So wise you are in the ways of love?"

"It's something Tieresias told me," Ismene admitted.

"Oh, I know that old bird was once a peacock...," Haemon laughed again.

"I wish I would have known him....her. You know, he was a woman. It was Hera who turned her into a man."

"I have heard the story," Haemon frowned. "It's one of his better tales."

"He says life is better as a woman...," Ismene frowned." I do not see how it can be better. We are the pawns of men."

"And men think just the opposite."

Haemon was walking faster. Moving into areas of darkness. Ismene had trouble adjusting her eyes to see the pathway.

"How can you know where you are headed?" she asked. His hand reached out to steady her as she stumbled over rocks.

"My mother hid herself in the depths of even Death. I have learned the path after many a fall," Haemon murmured. He took her hand in his.

"How did you know where to find her the first time?"

"Hades told me. He felt I had the right to know...."

"Hades," Ismene repeated the name. The god of death, who seemed more alive than any here. She thought on him. His dark twisted locks, his eyes that swallowed light, and his anger flowing through him as surely as blood in her veins. It did not seem in Hades's nature to be immediately kind, and yet, he had concerned himself with Haemon's sorrow. His frown impressed itself upon her as deeply as his sudden smile.

Again, she walked in silence, thinking on Hades. How could his wife forget him even there in the bountiful earth above? Such love and such patience to wait for Perserphone again and again through the dance of years. Perhaps that was the greatest romance of all, the romance of a god who longed for a wife who did not return his affections.

They walked for a time in silence. Haemon guided her gently through the darkness.

"Will we be able to see her when we arrive?" Ismene asked.

"There are sulfurous fires there that make everything red. You will see her...." As he spoke she saw ahead a crimson point that began to fan out as they approached it.

"This is where the wretched go to cry and wail throughout eternity. Those that will not be comforted…," Haemon explained. "Your mother once asked me where my mother was. I lied; said I did not know. You must lie, too, if she asks you. They loved each other like sisters when alive. Your mother would not want to see Eurydice in such a state."

"It is as Tieresias once said when I asked him what it was like to be blind," Ismene said sadly. Haemon turned to her. "He said we were all blind in some way about some thing."

"Oh, Tieresias had an answer for everything," Haemon touched her hand lightly. "If he had kept quiet once in a while, he might still be living at the palace."

"I like his voice better than his silence," Ismene was suddenly angry. Tieresias had been her only comfort in those years after Oedipus died. When she had returned with Antigone, Creon took them in to his court, but he did not welcome them into his heart. Eurydice was kind to Ismene, but Antigone fought with everyone. Except Haemon. Haemon seemed to know how to calm her. Was that love? Ismene determined to ask Hades when she next saw him, he who protested the great love he felt for Perserphone.

"You must sit here until I tell my mother of your circumstances," Haemon instructed. "She is not used to any visitors except myself."

"She is alone?" Ismene looked ahead at the great red rise of flames.

"She prefers it."

Haemon pushed her shoulder as he answered, leaving Ismene alone on a rock. She watched Haemon step carefully into the fiery setting. The wails of those who lived there touched her ears like angry fingers. Suddenly Ismene felt immensely hungry. She realized she had not eaten since the morning. This world was not a world where her needs were so quickly honored. She was dependent on Hades and his kindnesses. *Patience?* Tieresias must have meant her patience. As she sat, her stomach rumbling, she became aware of a shadow moving towards her. It was the young girl, Umbra, carrying a basket.

"Here I find you. Finally! Hades wants you to stay in one place. I cannot be searching for you…." So saying, Umbra placed the basket at Ismene's feet.

"Hades thought of me," Ismene spoke in surprise.

"Be glad he did think of you. There would be no other way for you to keep on living...."

"Tell him I return the favor and think of him...."

Umbra looked as though she might laugh.

"Do you think a god cares whether you think of him?"

"Nonetheless, I do. And with gratitude." With that, Ismene reached into the basket, drawing forth a piece of fruit. The sweetness of the juice filled her mouth as she bit into it. Never had such sweetness filled her before! With a short gasp, she looked up, but Umbra was gone. Another taste of the fruit. Ismene reached for the small jar of lentils, emptying them into her devouring mouth. Then the bread, crisply chewed. Blessed, blessed life! Here even in the extremes of the Netherworld, life could be worshipped. She suddenly knew she was very young, and this Kingdom of Death was not for her. Was that what Tieresias wanted her to understand? Her choices should lead her to the fullness of each day, not to the diminishment. Her belly full, tears running down her cheeks, she saw the flame of Eurydice running towards her. Haemon stood back and let his mother embrace Ismene. Ismene knew she had come to the end of her descent. Anything after this would lift her up again.

Part Two:
The Climb Back

"I must conquer this wish to die, to be punished as my family has been punished for the curse put on us so long ago." Ismene spoke these words when left alone by Haemon. She was standing by the great lake, looking into its depths, contemplating her own face. The face of a young woman.

"Is this what your day teaches you?" She turned to find Hades watching her.

"Yes. I am not ready to be a shade."

"So you are hungry for more than food?" His mouth played with a smile.

"Haemon took me to the end regions of your kingdom."

"Yes, I know," Hades nodded. "I know where you are. I must know. You almost got away today, but then I looked at the very place you should not be."

"And there I was."

She stood for a long moment silently examining this strange god. He seemed at once interested and disinterested in her.

"Creon's soldiers are still searching for you. Even at the gates of Corinth.. I came to the King of Corinth in a dream to warn him as you wished."

"I am pleased. I hope he takes the warning."

"It is, as Tieresias told you, a matter of patience."

Ismene moved closer to him. His black eyes shone like polished marble. "I thought he meant that you, Hades, must have patience."

47

"Perhaps the meaning is different for each of us. Tieresias has been known to speak puzzles...."

She was silent again, caught by his gaze. When this god was moved to passion did his eyes change?

"Can I dine with you tonight?" her invitation came out boldly.

He moved away. "No, Ismene. I am in mourning."

"As I said...," she followed him. "You are in mourning for one who is living and destined to return to you. A useless exercise in tears."

His back to her, he stopped. "I know you are lonely here. Even with your family. Their concerns are no longer your concerns. But I am not a good companion for so young a maiden."

"You are not used to being sought out for company," she surmised. His back shook slightly. "The dead fear you. You have power over their time here. All the time....the living fear you, too. You will be their king at their most dreaded moment. I have decided to cheer you up."

His back shook more. She realized he was laughing.

"You give me no recourse except patience. Otherwise, I would have to punish you for speaking so to me...."

"I am lonely." Her voice was no more than a breath.

"As am I," Hades acknowledged. "I will send for you soon, but not tonight."

He continued to walk, vanishing along the twisted corridors beyond the lake.

Ismene moved the other way, towards the aperture opening into her family's dwelling. Antigone met her at the door.

"We sought for you everywhere." Antigone's voice had its scolding quality that used to frighten Ismene. Now Ismene took her sister's hand, leading them both within. Haemon was sitting with Oedipus, throwing dice. Jocasta polished a mirror.

"Remember, family, that I have no task here other than to hide. One day, I will be called back, and none of you will find me," Ismene spoke pleasantly. Haemon looked up with a frown.

"You should tell us gossip from the world above us...." Jocasta always had loved gossip.

"I will do so, mother, if you tell me gossip from this world. Tieresias will expect me to know what has happened here. He is almost as fond of gossip as yourself...."

The stories were exchanged, some punctuated with laughter or tears. Both worlds were divested of their trivial secrets.. At last. Ismene begged the right to sleep. She went into the inner chamber, crawled on the ledge, and dreamed her first dream of love. The man in the dream was faceless. His hands moved gently through the lovemaking. In the morning. she found her time of bleeding had begun. In the world above, there would have been some ritual, but here, she tore her blue garment to make rags to stop the stain.

* * *

When she awoke Umbra was standing over her with a basket of food, a jar of fresh water, and a clean garment.

"You slept late," Umbra said. Her face was shaped into a disapproving frown. Ismene sat up quickly.

"I am tired. Humans get tired. I assume the dead do not."

Umbra shrugged.

"When you have eaten and washed, clap your hands. Hades wishes you to accompany him today."

Ismene quickly felt wide awake. "Where is he taking me?"

"Do not be so inquisitive. He goes a great many places. You will be his companion." So saying, Umbra left the inner chamber.

Ismene ate hurriedly. The excitement flushed her cheeks as she washed and braided her long hair. Tearing up the rest of her blue garment for rags, she suddenly blushed. Hades must have known it was her time of moon! He had provided a new robe for her to wear. This robe was dark brown like the cave floors. Of course! His wife was mortal and therefore subject to bleeding at the same phase of the moon. Looking at herself in the fragmented crystals of the chamber walls, Ismene judged she looked attractive enough for even a god. She clapped her hands in delight. Immediately, there was the sound of a great wind.

"Come out from there." She recognized Hades's voice. "I do not set even my toe into the chamber of a maiden."

After her dream the night before, she did not feel as though she were still a maiden, but Ismene obeyed this strange god, emerging into the main chamber of the cave. He wore a long black cloak covering his body. In spite of herself, she admired his wonderful midnight eyes and hair, his silver skin, and his great height.

"I hope, Hades, I will prove a good companion to you today." Her words sounded foolish as soon as she spoke them.

"We will ride out into the heavens today."

"Do we go to Olympus?"

"No," he thundered his reply." I have no wish for the company of my brother who exiled me here. He gives me permission only rarely to travel outside this world. I want to go far....and show you something of a life beyond your own."

"Would Tieresias approve?"

"You are still a child to ask approval of a blind old man! Dare to this adventure."

Tears stung her eyes. Yes, he thought of her as a child, to be threatened with punishments. She would show him that her maidenhood was nearing its end. She would not be the girl who waited outside the oracle's cave while her father heard his fate within.

"How do we travel?"

"I will show you...." He extended his hand. His touch chilled her more deeply than any other touch she had yet received, and yet she did not withdraw her hand. He suddenly pulled her very quickly with him to the opening of the Netherworld. Cerberus sat patiently as Hades petted him. Then as quickly as he had pulled her, he lifted her high in the air. For a moment, she thought he would drop her, but he set her down on the back of a dragon who lay crouched. Then he slung his leg carelessly across the dragon.

"Hold on to my waist," he commanded. She grabbed him with the sum of all her fear and excitement, her head resting against his strong back. As the dragon rose into the sky, she gave a small cry.

"Are you afraid?" he asked.

"No. It is not fear that I feel....something else I have never felt."

Then they were both quiet as the world disappeared into clouds and a darkness blacker than night held in place by pins of stars.

"There has been no one for so long to make this ride," he sighed.

"Your wife…"

"My wife is of the earth, bound to the soil. She does not like this ocean of air that heaves and swells beyond…." At that moment, Ismene looked down to see a circle of white.

"That is our world?" she asked. "I thought it would be flat…."

"Curved…like the mountains, like the shape of fruit, like the lips of the lover, the curl of waves, the breasts of…," Hades stopped.

"Oh go on! You are speaking poetry!"

"I speak of things beyond your years."

"You put far too much value on my maidenhood," she snapped.

"And you put far too little," he returned. Then they were quiet, taking in the rush of other worlds passing them. Comets approached in fiery curiosity.

"Even Olympus must seem small to you when you ride here," Ismene said at last.

"I used to ride here often with my two brothers, but now they are afraid of leaving their thrones for fear they will be deposed as they once deposed our father. I lost companions…"

"I too made many journeys with Antigone which she no longer wanted to make once she fell in love with Haemon. Then I had to go alone…." Ismene's voice trailed off after she remembered her last journey with Antigone and Oedipus, which had restored his sanity after Jocasta's suicide.

"Sad memories," Hades remarked simply.

"Why did you decide to bring me with you?" Ismene asked after a long moment when a comet passed before them.

"You were right to remind me, I mourn someone not dead."

Suddenly, aromas began to rise from Hades, reminding Ismene of the herbs used to prepare dead bodies. She began to recognize these smells as arising from him when strong emotions overtook him. She had smelled them before.

"Mourning was too strong a word. I know you must miss her," Ismene said.

The aromas increased, making her dizzy with their essence.

"I miss her less today," he whispered.

"Then you should ride your dragon here more often. The universe reminds us how small we are....even gods."

"Yes," he moved quickly, almost upsetting her hold on him. He was reining in the dragon. Ahead, there was a sphere. Coming closer, Ismene saw the shape of a red ocean with an azure beach. Beyond that, the horizon looked like a woven cloth.

"Are we stopping?" she asked.

"This is the end of the universe. There is no where to go beyond this point." The dragon floated down to the blue sands. Hades dismounted and quickly, easily, picked Ismene up in his arms.

"I did not know the universe had an end...."

"I discovered it only a few centuries ago. Athena was here. She tore away part of the netting...."

Ismene was set on her feet. The azure sands moved to adjust to her. "We are held in a net?"

"No, we are part of a series of strings....all woven together and pulled this way or that to make the illusion of a world. It is not easy to understand. Athena did not understand...."

Athena was the goddess of wisdom, sprung from the aching head of Zeus one day. If she did not understand, how could Ismene comprehend?

"She tore the netting by mistake. With her arrow. There was a great disturbance suddenly, even as far as our world. Earthquakes and the spitting of fires from mountains. Zeus threatened to imprison her, but her sister, Artemis, who relies not on wisdom but intuition, came to her defense, tied the netting together, and saved her sibling."

"I have never heard of this! "Ismene cried.

"It is not part of the stories we let humans tell. And you are sworn to secrecy...." Hades shook his finger.

"The gods are as petty as humans," Ismene touched his finger with her own.

"The understanding of strings as the basis for the universe comes to you much later in time. We gods keep our secrets....but not forever. Someday, you will have no use for us. You will ride to these shores, but on quite different dragons. Then we will sit together and tell our old tales as warriors do. To remind ourselves we were once invincible."

"And beyond the universe?"

Hades looked at her with sorrow. "I do not know what is beyond this universe. Perhaps another. With other petty gods trying to hold sway over the petty lesser images that populate it."

"You are very cynical."

"I am old. You are young. When you live your long length of years, we will meet again...."

Ismene thought of herself as an old woman who could not mount the great flying dragon. An old woman who would sit in the sulfurous center with Eurydice and keen to the accompaniment of the dark fires there.

"I am glad I will see you again one day when you will not treat me like a silly child," Ismene said at last.

"And when you will treat me with more respect," Hades replied.

Looking on his silver face of sorrow, Ismene thought respect was not the first attitude she would take. She wanted to touch him, smooth away the pain, spread his lips in a smile. She often wanted the same effect from Tieresias when she would meet him at the edge of his eyrie. Sometimes he would seem happy by the time she left to return to Creon's palace.

"I would like to put my toes in that ocean," she tried a light voice.

"You are free to walk the shoreline. I will rest here with my dragon."

"You won't come with me?"

"I will enjoy watching you enjoy yourself," Hades said. As he spoke, she smelled the scents again, this time of sweet fruits. It was as good for her as any smile he might bestow.

She said no more but moved into the water, lifting the bottom of her robe, and feeling the strange liquid touch of the red caress her legs. In the distance, behind Hades and his dragon, were rocks that bit into the sky like broken teeth in a multitude of colors. Everything was displaced here in the way she was displaced in the land of death.

What did this displacement signify? Death or life? There were no plants, no flying creatures, no fish in the ocean. Only herself, the god of death, and a dragon powerful enough to bring them here. She tried to imagine Athena walking in the water, the same way she walked. Athena, she had seen at a small overgrown temple, in statue form. The marble face was thin and severe. Not a goddess to frolic on the beaches of time. Perhaps a woman with an angry temper. Perhaps the divine counterpart to Antigone. Was Ismene then like Athena's sister, Artemis? From representations she had seen of Artemis, the goddess was less perfect looking, less divine. The oily hair and feral smile of this goddess linked her to the animals and elements of woodlands. No, it was vain to compare one's self even to the qualities (if not the appearance) of a goddess. Ismene preferred to think herself naught but a young maiden who might be anyone, wading in waters that promised pleasure. The red of the waters prompted her to remember her time of blood. A time of change.

Hades was lying now against the dragon. His eyes were closed. She looked at him without censor. Perhaps if he had been a prince from another kingdom in another life, her father would have betrothed her to him. Perhaps he would have been the man to mimic her dream last night.

"Perhaps," she said to herself softly, "he would see me with the eyes of a man in love..." Then abruptly, she sighed. Hades was already in love. He had chosen. Some would say he had not chosen wisely, but wisdom had little part in choices of the heart. Athena, Wisdom's goddess, was a virgin. Aphrodite was the love goddess, quite different.

She turned away from Hades, towards the line of the shore. Small perfect waves broke against her bare legs. Once, she and Antigone had spent a day with their nurse by the great waters laughing over the persistence of the waves. Once, her mother had pulled her from a lake. Ismene could not swim. Water had never been her friend. Creon, when angry, threatened to drown her more than once.

Now she was washed in fear. She ran from the water onto the safety of the blue beach. She had walked a great distance. Hades was awaking. He stretched his arms and called to her.

"I will not let him see my fear," she decided. She wondered as she returned to him whether she had a smell that would give her away just as he had. From where he stood, the sweetness of the fruits still emanated.

"You will eat now," he ordered, "and then we will return."

"We cannot stay until nighttime?" she begged.

"There is no nighttime here." He pulled a cloth from beneath his cloak. As she reached for it, he withdrew his arm. "No. This is my food. You eat otherwise…," and he gave her a small baked loaf.

"We cannot eat the same food?"

"I eat ambrosia and drink nectar. Here is a jug of wine for you."

"May I taste…?"

"No!" said Hades, so definitively she did not argue. Her loaf tasted good enough, and the wine made her head spin.

"Now," he said when they had finished, each eating in a self-enclosed silence. He put his arms about her waist and lifted her onto the dragon. She could hardly wait for him to mount so that she might put her arms about him. *Was this love?* Once, Orpheus had sung at her father's court. She remembered only a tatter of the song:

> *Love breaks the vessel*
> *to hold the liquid*
> *more securely*
> *that could spill*
> *and vanish.*
> *Love is the emptiness*
> *within the cup,*
> *filling up*
> *of Itself.*

That night, she sat on Tieresias's lap as she listened to the beautiful voice enchant everyone. Later, Tieresias walked her to her chamber saying, "Memory will keep this song until time explains it."

"But," she thought, "I cannot be in love with the god of death!"

She suddenly recalled that Tieresias once told her she would speak with Hades and more. Tieresias had promised Ismene that her contact with Hades would surprise even the Oracle of Delphi. What more might happen? Already, she had traveled with Hades to the end of the universe, walked in a sea of scarlet, and ridden back to the land of Death upon a great dragon. The excitement made her tremble.

"Are you cold?" Hades asked, feeling her small shaking body against his own.

"No, it is nothing," she breathed. *It was everything! To have shared such a great adventure!*

The dragon floated into the opening of the Netherworld just as the sun was lowering into the cloud banks. Hades lifted her quickly to the ground.

"By now, you should know your way back to your family," he said.

"Thank you for taking me with you today." He nodded his head and turned to go.

"I will never forget this day," she added. She hoped he would stop, turn to her again, and continue speaking. Instead, he followed the path along the lake more quickly, his dragon behind him.

Ismene stood for a long time by the entrance to the Netherworld. Outside, Cerberus was growling and barking with his three heads at the bats that filled up the darkening skies. She felt no desire to sit among her family, answering their questions about her day. The day was best kept a secret one. Hades had imparted to her truths about the universe and gossip about the gods who ruled that universe. Ismene finally went into the large chamber with the great lake. She looked into the smooth water, seeing her face reflected.

"I have nothing of Artemis in me," she thought sadly. She brushed the water with her hand, rippling the image therein. "I am no goddess, but rather a silly girl who ran away from home." She wished Tieresias were there to console her, tell her stories of his/her wonderful life. Instead, she saw only a few figures lingering on the other side of the great room.

"Tonight I will stay with Eurydice," she determined, remembering the path she walked the day before with Haemon. "Eurydice will not ask questions. It was always her best quality. She let you tell her what you wished."

ISMENE: THE JOURNEY BACK

The walk to the center of the earth took some time, with a few deviations she needed to correct. Eurydice was waiting for her as she stumbled into the fiery core.

"How did you know I would come?" Ismene asked, amazed.

"I saw you in the flames. Perhaps Hades put your image there. You are under his protection," Eurydice smiled. "I have made a place for you here...." She gestured to a small ledge. "I am glad for the company."

"You wished to be here alone! Haemon told me!"

"Yes, most of the time. I am waiting for Creon, when he comes one day. I know he cannot be with the others. He has hurt them too deeply...."

Eurydice looked directly into Ismene's eyes. "He killed them."

"He wishes to kill me, too, Eurydice. That is why I am here....hiding among those already dead in order not to become the dead."

Eurydice's grey eyes stormed, although her voice was gentle, "Creon changed once he had real power. Death strips us of many qualities we add during life. It will diminish the king in him. I fell in love with a man, not a king. Everyone else will desert him. Someone must be there for his eternity."

"Is this love?" Ismene wondered aloud.

"Perhaps it is love. It is certainly my duty as a wife," Eurydice smiled. "And now, you should wash and change your garment. I believe you are passing the blood."

"It is the first time. Tieresias gave me a charm to delay my menses, but I left it when I fled the palace. He felt Creon would harm me if he knew I were able to bleed with the moon's turning. Because that meant I could conceive. Creon fears more of our house."

Eurydice nodded, helping Ismene off with her garments. They filled a bowl from a spring that bubbled even in the world of fire. Ismene stood while Eurydice smoothed the water over her skin.

"You are growing into a lovely woman, Ismene," Eurydice remarked, standing back to look on her.

"Not compared to Antigone. Antigone was the beautiful one," Ismene protested.

"That was when you were a gangly girl, but now you are a rival even for Antigone."

Ismene looked on Eurydice with eyes of admiration. This woman who was willing to endure isolation even in death that she might await her husband, a man reviled by all her family! This woman had qualities Ismene hoped to possess one day—loyalty and deep love. Eurydice always had an innate elegance, to which was added royalty, but here was some quality greater than those two. Eurydice had acquired divinity for Ismene.

"You flatter me, Eurydice. The most beautiful woman in life or death is yourself....your face is a study of a woman who has lived her life and beyond without dishonesty." *Was this what Tieresias meant by patience? Patience,* thought Ismene, *was just the impulse of the person. But how did one decide where patience was needed? Who was worthy of patience?*

Eurydice was handing her a goblet.

"Umbra brought this just before you came to find me. She said Hades wishes you to drink the draught. That is how I knew you were coming to find me."

"I thought you saw me in the flames...."

"Look into the cup...." Ismene looked into the churning liquid of the cup and saw flames arising there with faces from her past. Tieresias's face surfaced on the lapping of orange.

"Umbra brings what Hades wishes...," murmured Ismene. She took a long sip from the frothing beverage. Suddenly, she was filled with a heaviness that she could not fight. Eurydice caught her as she swayed.

"It cannot be poison. There is no poison in this land of death," Eurydice cried.

"Not poison, but I will sleep...." Ismene's eyes were already closing. "You need not watch over me. I am protected...."

Her sleep was fitful as the universe she had witnessed with the sudden arc of comets, the fiery stars, the distant worlds with colors that did not match what she knew of sky or land or even shape of surface. In spite of the disturbances, she felt the eyes of Hades upon her, watching out for her safety. His dragon breathed a flaming trail behind the god, but Hades would not let the dragon come too close to Ismene. In her dream, she asked him how it was he showed such concern for her, and at the same time, such irritation. He did not answer but kept his silence as sentry over her. Then she saw the eyeless gaze of her father and the wisdom of Tieresias's look that could tell her feelings without need of eyes or hands or even voice. To Tieresias, she tried to run, pleading, "Take me out of here! I am in danger!" And she knew the danger came not from Creon and his soldiers. The danger was the danger of her own heart beating wildly in a world where hearts had stopped. What right had she to come to this world? What right had she to feel these feelings for a god? A god who loved another mortal?

Abruptly, Ismene awoke, sitting up, to find Eurydice patiently stroking her head.

"I did need to watch over you," Eurydice said. "You cried out many times in your sleep. You did the same as a child. Your mother and nurse thought you were trying to get their attention, but I knew you suffered from bad dreams. I would often sit by you until the dawn. With the sunlight, the dreams went away...."

"Yes, what I need is sunlight. I miss many things in this world, but sunlight, I miss the most, next to Tieresias." Ismene began to cry.

"You feel more deeply than most other people...," Eurydice mused. "The land of the dead is no place for such a woman."

"You called me a woman!" Ismene smiled.

"Your blood is running. You are a woman," Eurydice nodded. "You should not be here. What was Tieresias thinking?"

"He wanted me to learn patience. It is often my impatience that lands me in danger. Creon knew that. He..." she stopped, her eyes wide.

"Creon knew you did not have the soul of a prisoner," Eurydice smiled. "None of your family does. That is why Oedipus put out his eyes and left the city, why Jocasta hung herself. They would have been prisoners in the palace afterwards."

"Everyone left me in one way or another. Even you, Eurydice."

"Forgive me, Ismene."

Ismene shook her head, rising and walking towards the spring to wash herself for her next day here. *A day! What marked her life as a day where no sun rose or set? How long was a day here?* As she shook the water over her body, she tried to think how Hades endured his sentence to guard and rule over the dead. He must be the very model of patience, waiting only for the coming of his wife to change the long arc of time. From his own lips, she had heard his resentment that he was given this charge by his brothers who assigned their rule to kingdoms of heavens, earth, and sea, where seasons were marked and worlds shifted. She thought of his tense excited muscles against her body as they flew through the sky on his dragon. He must have been a high-strung, heady lad. Now he was older, more placid in his nature. His one rebellion had been to marry someone forbidden to him. It was enough. He was forever marked among the gods to remain singular and apart. Why had not Persephone conceived? A child of his would give him companionship, help him through this banishment. Perhaps her mother, Demeter, had given her herbs to help stave off a pregnancy. Tieresias often did the same for girls who were desperate enough to climb up to his eyrie, threatening to end their lives if he did not help them.

Sitting there braiding her long hair, Ismene wondered what Perspehone thought of this god. The violence of his taking her marred her vision. Or perhaps she had given her own heart to someone else who was forever denied her after Hades marked her for his own.

"I will ask Tieresias when I return," Ismene said aloud. "You inquire too deeply," a voice behind her said. She rose, recognizing Umbra's disapproving tone. "It is not for you to question so much of the world. It will not lead to happiness."

"It is the way I am made." Ismene pulled on her robes.

"Hades wishes for you to join him now." Umbra turned and began to walk away. After a second, she looked back. "You will follow me."

Ismene followed silently. She did not trust herself with Hades, but Tieresias had instructed her to humor Hades always.

"I must learn the patience of my own passions," she thought as she walked behind the quick-paced Umbra along the dark passage that led up towards the great lake. Haemon passed her, coming down to see his mother.

"Ismene! We were worried....no one knew where you went...."

"I have been with Eurydice. There is no more I can say now....Hades requests my presence...." Ismene managed a small smile. She had always liked Haemon, who had more time for her than many lads his age. In some ways, she felt closer to him than to Antigone, who took an imperious tone with her younger sister.

"Come back to us this evening. We miss you...," he called.

Ismene knew that any life inserted into this kingdom was appreciated. She breathed and slept and ate and changed. These were actions of the living. Everyone else here was frozen. Perhaps, even in death, the thought of ageing was comforting.

"Speed your steps!" Umbra commanded.

Ismene gave Haemon a short wave and moved faster, stumbling over the stones on the pathway. Umbra on the other hand floated smoothly. Being no more than a shadow, she had a grace that a living person lacked. They had reached the great lake. Umbra touched a large boulder, which moved aside.

"Go in," she said, giving Ismene a small push.

Within, was a cave with smoothed crystal walls. Hades was standing to one side, his face heavy with care.

"I wish you would not think on me quite so much. It keeps me from my work...." His voice was thick.

"And what is your work?" Ismene demanded.

"My work is..." he stopped. "I must listen for signals from the other gods to help the universe turn."

"I would not think of you, except that you keep sending for me. Inserting yourself in my thoughts," came her quick reply. *It was true!* In spite of himself, he sought her company.

His face was poised exactly between a smile and a frown. Then he took her by the shoulders and stood her in front of him.

"This is the room where we can see what is happening above. You brought me here with your imploring concerning Creon's invasion."

"Then he has invaded?"

Her eyes examined the shiny walls. The longer she looked, the clearer the images were. She saw Creon in his chariot with his army behind him, the devastation of the borders of Corinth.

"You must look more deeply yet," Hades whispered.

"You said you did not like to come into this room..." Ismene accused.

"I was forced to come by your words. I had to see if my warning to the king had any effect...." It was at that moment, she saw the wise wizened face of Corinth's king. He, too, was in his chariot with his army behind him, moving towards the Theban border.

"He did heed your warning."

"Yes, much good it will do him. Now he faces slaughter." The god of death closed his eyes. "Why do men not learn?"

"Perhaps he will win...."

"Look at Creon's armies...." She saw a vast panorama of men. "And look at your king...." The army's ranks were far fewer and badly armed.

"Did you bring me here, Hades, to watch men die?"

"Of course I did not. I know you have seen all you wish to see of death. You are living among the dead."

Yes, she thought, but they are already dead. They are not filled with life and air in their lungs, racing towards what they hope is glory only to fall on the battlefield. So it was with her brothers! Two braggarts on the most glorious morning imaginable in a rush to their demise.

"Why did you bring me here?"

"Tieresias has been on these walls...."

"Oh!" she gave a small cry, rushing to touch her fingers to the clear sides of the cave. "I missed him." She put her head against the cool surface as though she might push her way through, back to the land of the living.

"He asked for you...."

Ismene tried to hold back tears. "I wanted to see him. How I miss him!"

"He will show his image again."

Her one hand wiped away the tears that flooded over her face.
"I need him. I need his counsel."

Hades shifted on his feet impatiently. "This was not a good idea, hiding you here."

"Why? I was safe here."

"Safe from what? From whom? You are seeing what a living maiden should never see."

"My family as mere shells of what they were? I know what happens in death. I cannot change…"

"No, not that!" His irritation made her tears stop. She stood up straight, her eyes distracted from the images of the world beyond. "You are seeing beyond the moment now. You are being cursed, like the oracle of Delphi, with a deeper sight."

"I see nothing more than what is right before my eyes."

"Do not toy with me. Your fate is one I recognize. Remember, I am a god. You are here to learn of a greater world than maidens know. A greater world than even your parents knew. No wife or mother will you be."

The line of anger behind his calm voice made her afraid.

"Tieresias sent me here to hide me…."

"And to reveal you as well. He spoke, for once, in a straightforward way. You will be summoned soon back to his eyrie. Creon will not harm you."

"I can leave…?" She looked into the ebony cast of his eyes which revealed nothing. He would not mourn her leaving as he mourned Perserphone. "I can go home…." Now she thought of Tieresias welcoming her into the familiar patterns of their time together.

"It will not be the same between the two of you," Hades said, as though he read her thoughts. "Tieresias cannot treat you as his daughter now. You will transform yourself in those coming days, as a worm becomes a butterfly."

"Will Creon be defeated in this battle we are watching?"

"In this battle, no. In the war, yes. Arrogance takes a man to a dangerous place. A pinnacle where no one else will stand. Creon will mount that pinnacle in his ego, and he will be toppled."

Eurydice even now was waiting to welcome her husband home to his final residence.

"You were right not to come to this room. It is a terrible room where one can see future hurts and defeats," Ismene murmured.

All around her, on the smooth walls, were reflected images of the world above them. Some of the pictures were happy ones of people in the fields or walking through the market places; some were of people sick or abandoned; some were the warriors going into battle.

"Such a small fragment of the larger universe," Hades said, giving voice to her thoughts.

"Why don't you show the dead what we saw during our ride? Why don't you put that on these walls?"

"Eventually people will know of that wider life. But slowly. We must bring them slowly from their absorption with themselves. Someday…"

"Who made people so selfish? Was it not the gods?" Ismene cried.

"And you know the gods are selfish as well…," Hades said. "Every last one of us. Why should people be made better than their deities?"

Ismene had a memory of the day she had walked with Tieresias along the edge of his cliff. She had held the clawlike hand of the prophet in her own. He stopped to take in a lungful of the thin air.

"Almost a perfect day. I think if I could see, the sun would stand alone in the blue sky without the shelf of clouds…."

Ismene had smiled, then put her head against his bony shoulder.

"I will never know such peace again," he said.

"Is this how gods and goddesses feel?" she questioned.

"Gods and goddesses can never feel this peace. They must always be wary. The world depends on them."

She looked at Hades now with the awareness that he must always walk a line between his emotions and his logic. Zeus had been known to incite catastrophes for mortals with his own quick anger. Poseiden had lost men at sea, submerged continents when his sea rage grew.

"I think you have taught me patience," she said in surprise, reaching out to Hades. He moved away, not letting her touch him.

"A strange lesson for one such as myself to teach," he replied.

"Not strange at all. Why can't you acknowledge you can demonstrate good?"

"I am the god of death. What could be more negative?"

"Or more satisfactory? It is the end of living on the earth. That is all. Those who feared life will fear you. That is not your fault...."

She wanted to rock him in her arms, the way she had rocked some of the children in the palace who cried.

He moved further away as though discerning her thoughts.

"You cannot stop me from caring for you, Hades, however far away you step...." Her voice was gentle. "I have come..."

"Do not say it! I forbid you!" His voice was harsh. "You are not to love me."

"Because of your wife?"

"Because of yourself. It is never a good choice to love a god."

"I do not get to choose whom I love. Love is not something that one can learn in the same way one can learn to count. If I should love you, it does not mean any obligation on your part." Her voice was cool as the rain.

"You are leaving here. All mortals who have not died must leave. They must, if only to fill their lungs with the atmosphere of the living. I cannot follow. Maybe for a day, maybe for two, but I have to return. A king cannot leave his people, even those beyond the oxygen of life."

"Yes," she nodded sadly, "I am required to leave. To return to my world. To take up where Tieresias cannot." It was the first time she realized her heritage came from Tieresias, not Oedipus. "But I know a few truths. I will understand the oracle of Delphi when I return because of what I learned here in your kingdom. And Tieresias told me I would do more than merely speak with you...."

She understood finally it was her coming to love Hades that expanded her knowledge of the world. It was not enough to love a mortal man. That might have led her to children and a quiet hearth. Hades took her on a ride to the edge of the universe, a love song no mortal man could sing to her. The consummation of her love for this god was not the exercise of the lesson. The lesson was in the loving.

"You can continue to talk to me as a child….but I am not a child. It is as a woman I wish to be accepted or rejected by you."

His back was against the wall of the cave. The images of the cave retreated.

"How can I accept you?" His voice was heavy with pain. "I have a wife, and you are to return to your world. I would not even have six moons of you."

"The very fact that you are in torment puts me in torment. I would never wish to put you there. I will stay away from you until I leave…."

Tears ran along her face.

"But it is I who seek you out. It is I who make demands…."

"You are lonely to talk with another mortal when Perserphone is away. I remind you of her…."

"You are nothing like her. She is cool where you push at me. She would never care about my pain…."

Ismene's arms ached to hold him. "Then she is a fool. for all that you love her!"

Hades took a step towards her. "Take me to the edges of *your* universe, Ismene. Ride me there. Let me be the pupil….the child."

And she folded him into her embrace. The cold touch of him became warm in her arms. Her lips pushed against his until his mouth opened to her. Nothing could cure this thirst for him, not even consummation. She felt his hands on her breasts with a spring of surprise. He laid her on the floor of the cave.

"Tell me what I should do for you," he whispered.

"We will do it together. First you to me, then I to you."

Although she had never made love, she remembered Antigone's confidences of how Haemon tongued Antigone into ecstasy. And how Antigone returned the ecstasy to him with careful dances of lips. And so the lovemaking began.

* * *

The sulfur fires rose up around her as she went to find Eurydice. She was still adjusting her robes, touching her skin to be sure the fires were without not within. Somehow, she knew Tieresias had knowledge of her encounter. It made her blush.

"Ismene." Eurydice's voice stopped her.

"I came to be with you one more time." Ismene tried to keep her voice light.

"Then you are leaving?"

"I must leave, Eurydice. No mortal can stay eternally in the kingdom of Hades until their death."

Eurydice took both Ismene's hands, staring intently into the face of the girl.

"Will you say no farewell to your family?"

"Of course I will. But first to you." Ismene tried to return the steady gaze. "I will say farewell to all who will miss me...." Inwardly, she thought of Hades standing half in the dark of the corridor outside the room of visions. His eyes glowed much as two coals. He was not smiling, but she knew he looked upon her with an affection that was much like—if not—love itself. There would be a farewell with him.

"I feel when I will see you again you will be a very old woman," Eurydice said.

"Yes." Ismene imagined herself there in the future returning across the water in Charon's boat. "I will be a crone." *Would Hades desire her then?*

"And a very great woman." Eurydice kissed her gently.

Ismene turned and made her way up the incline from the sulphurous fires to her family's cave. They were sitting in the half-light of the main chamber. Her father and mother had their hands entwined. Antigone was teasing Haemon.

"Where have you been? We were worried!" her mother chided her.

"I am fine, mother. How could I be harmed here?"

"You are leaving us," said her father, who always knew her better.

"Yes, I think Creon is distracted with his war. He always must make wars, you know. Tieresias has called me home...," her voice lingered on the word 'home'. She thought of the eyrie where Tieresias dwelled when she thought of home.

"And it will be a long time until you return," Antigone stated flatly.

"Yes, sister, a very long time."

They drew her into their wide embrace, reluctant to part with her not only because she was of them, but she was alive, warm to the touch. She was their reminder of a full life.

"I have one more farewell to make," she sighed, extracting herself from their arms.

"It is to Hades,"Oedipus said.

"Yes, father. I must thank the god of the dead for hiding me here. He might have refused."

"He would never refuse Tieresias," Haemon observed.

Reluctantly, Ismene left them. She made her way to the Chamber which was the throne room of the god she loved.

He was sitting on a rock-carved throne.

"I am in love with death," she said, kneeling before him.

"And I am in love with you," he returned.

"And yet we must part. Just as you part with Perserphone."

His eyes shut in a measure of pain.

"Unlike Perserphone, you will not return every six months. I cannot argue for you as I did for her."

"Then we must make this farewell last...I do not wish to leave here a maiden."

She was clasped to him as he kissed on every part of her, before he carried her into his inner chamber.

"I am in love with life," he murmured. "You are that life I love."

It was her gift to him, to his sorrow. For a moment, he cried out in joy. She cried out directly afterwards. Her joy which had not entered her being for so long rose up as a voice and shouted. When it was over, they slept in each other's arms. As though they would never part. As though this was the ending of a day together.

* * *

When she awoke, she was covered in Hades's black robe. She sat up abruptly, looking for him, but he was gone from the chamber. A moment later, Umbra floated in, carrying a platter of food and a goblet of wine.

"Charon is waiting for you. Hades thought you should eat before you began your journey back...." Umbra had the same disapproving tone she always used with Ismene.

"Hades does not wish to see me?" cried Ismene.

"No." It was flat and definite. Ismene pulled the black robe tighter around her. Her body still had the echoes of her pleasure.

"Would you tell the King of the Dead how..." she could not find the word... "how important this time was for me. I thank him for sheltering me." She felt the shelter in the garment around her. His smell like the funeral herbs embraced her.

"I will relay your message," came Umbra's prim reply.

Ismene wished Umbra to leave, but the shadowy figure lingered.

"I am here to help you prepare yourself," Umbra said at last.

"That, I can manage by myself."

Umbra bowed her head and was gone. Ismene realized she was naked beneath the robe. She found her garments and dressed quickly, drinking the wine and chewing on the bread as she did so. She was suddenly ravenous. There was a pool at the bottom of one wall where she washed herself. Perserphone must have done the same after nights of lovemaking. Hades would not have left his wife with no word. Tears began to run down Ismene's face in spite of her desire to hold on to the happiness. Braiding her hair, she folded the black robe, bringing it to her face one last time to inhale the smells of Hades. Outside, Umbra waited for her.

"Follow me," Umbra spoke with little inflection.

Ismene made her way out of the world of the dead with so little ceremony, it was as if she had never been there at all. The old ferryman was waiting beside Cerberus.

"About time," was all he said. Cerberus gave a mournful wail. Ismene reached out to smooth the fur of his massive body.

"I've never seen him do that," Charon spoke in surprise.

69

"I am friends with death," was all the explanation Ismene offered. She took the next few steps to the river bank and climbed into the boat. Something in her life had opened, but more of her life had closed. How could she ever be content with a mortal after Hades? She wondered where he was and why he was withholding himself from this farewell.

"Of course," she thought. "He has seen too many farewells with Perserphone. Farewells are not unique for him."

Charon began to pole the boat out onto the surface of the great river. The fog closed walls around them as the boat moved forward.

"You look sad," Charon observed. "Perserphone never does. She sits forward on her heels in anticipation."

"Someday, you will take me back across the Styx, when there is no possibility of return. Then I will sit on my heels full of anticipation...."

"Will it be soon?"

"I think not, although no person knows the moment of their death. Not even my father, to whom it was foretold...."

After that, they were silent until the opposite riverbank touched the boat's side. She did not know how much of human time had passed since she had first entered the Nether Kingdom, but as she climbed from the boat, she saw the flowers of the riverbank starting to bow their blossoms close to the ground. Soon, a chill would cover the land. Perserphone would wait anxiously on the riverbank for her journey back. And how would Hades greet her? It was with physical pain that Ismene thought of his lips sweeping those of his wife.

Charon offered her his hand as she stepped on to the ground. She nodded her head slightly in acknowledgment. She held the black robes of Hades in her arms. Perhaps she should return the garment, but then she thought it was all of him left for her to remember. Like a widow at the funeral pyre, she walked, her head high with the pride of one who had lost a great lover. Her steps took her back over the terrain where she had run before. Without thinking, she made her way to the cliffside of Tieresias's residence. She knew with certainty that he was waiting for her, leaning on his wooden stick, looking with his blind eyes over a landscape he could not see. This time, she did not fear Creon's soldiers. This time, she feared nothing except her own heart, which had almost undone her there in the subterranean kingdom.

* * *

He was there as she had foreseen him, waiting at the end of the long winding path that made its way up the hillside. It was almost dusk. "Welcome, Ismene." His voice comforted her as she fell into his arms.

"Oh Tieresias, what have you done to me! What adventures did you send me on!" His smell filled her.

"I did not make your adventures, my dear child. You made them for yourself. But I am a prophet and have the power to foresee outcomes...."

She began to laugh, her laughter circling them both like a songbird. "I thought I would be sadder," she said, at last.

"No, child, you bring back the joy you found there. It is odd to find joy in the Kingdom of Death, but you were always different than others."

"I need to tell you..." she drew back. "But then, you already know!"

"More than you do. I know you carry a child within you, half-formed as god and half as man."

"I did not think I would be a mother...."

"You will not. The babe must be returned to Hades when it is born. It cannot survive in our diminished world...."

"I cannot keep my child?"

"No. Too great a risk. Creon would hunt any child down. Hades will be comforted with this child...."

They stood for a moment in the rising wind. Again, the court of Artemis gathered in the sky.

"I want to go in," she said at last. "I am cold."

"Put on his robe. You will never be cold again," Tieresias spoke gently.

71

As she wound the robe about her, all the smells of his hair, his lips, his rich spill of semen filled her. He would have their child, but she would have this small occasion to bless the union of her heart. Maybe her only union.

* * *

She slept through the night and into the middle of the next day. Hades's robe enveloped her against the activity of Tieresias and the Thebans who made the journey up the hill to his world. They came in greater number now that Creon and his generals had gone to Corinth to fight. They came with requests they would never dare to make of their king. They came with need for charms against bad crops, poor sales of wheat, sickness, and the wrath of their enemies. Ismene woke to find them gathered around Tieresias. When they saw her, they moved away.

"I am not dead, citizens of Thebes," she spoke reassuringly.

"We were ordered to treat you as though you were, should you ever return," one small boy said at last.

"Princess, the king commanded your life be forfeit," an old woman spoke in a frightened voice.

"Then you must none of you tell King Creon she is here," Tieresias instructed them in his firm voice. Ismene remembered such a voice. He was not to be crossed when he spoke in it.

Ismene moved past them all onto the large ledge that overlooked the city. She found the little spring that was the source of water, washing her face and hands. Eventually, she shook out her blonde hair to the winds. The boy who spoke first came out to her with bread and fruit. He sat down, watching her as she ate.

"What is your name, child?" Ismene said when ignoring him no longer seemed an option.

"I am Xerxes." He smiled a small smile.

"Xerxes. Your father has a wife named Adriana. I know her." Ismene remembered the woman who had sold her beautiful feathers from another island so many years ago. The woman was pregnant, and Ismene remembered her telling Jocasta the child would be a healthy son named Xerxes.

"My father does not have such a wife." Xerxes moved away to swing on the low branch of a tree. "My mother died giving birth to me."

"I am sorry." Ismene knew that childbirth was as dangerous for a woman as war was for a soldier. She thought of the baby inside her, scarcely more than a mixture of the juices of love. Did Hades know about this baby? He had told her in the chamber of sight that she would be neither wife nor mother. Did he foresee she must give this child up?

Eventually Tieresias came out, telling Xerxes his family was leaving. Xerxes ran quickly to join them.

"Who cares for him now?" Ismene wondered.

"His aunt. Although she does it sparingly. He comes here for food and companionship many days. I think his father drinks most of the daylight away and snores most of the nighttime."

Tieresias sat down beside her in the bake of the late day.

"Why wouldn't Hades come to say farewell to me?" she had to ask.

"You will see him again…," Tieresias touched her blowing hair.

"I will see him again…," she repeated happily.

"You must not get mired in this love you feel," he warned her.

"I am not mired in it. I am impelled by it. I could not shake it off any more than I could shed my skin…."

"But you must. How else will you take on my role when I am gone?"

She pulled back to look into those sightless eyes.

"I cannot follow you, Tieresias. You are a great man, and I…" It was the first sign of real anger she had seen in the prophet since her childhood.. He shook her hard.

"Do not tell me what I know. I have seen it in the flames that you are to become what I am. I have seen it even through the veil placed on my eyes. Let us not waste time. You are no longer a child. As you told the mighty Hades!"

He had only been that angry with her once before, when she had killed a bird with a stone for sport. Then he had dragged her by her hair to the palace to her father's chamber and demanded that Oedipus punish her. Oedipus would not raise his hand to her, but Tieresias dragged her into the antechamber and beat her with his walking stick.

"You frighten me!" she cried out.

"I mean to frighten you…you are remembering the day I beat you?"

"Yes." After the beating she did not seek Tieresias out for six months.

"Tell me again you are a child…"

"No. I am not a child. I do not fear you for that reason. I have not your gifts."

"Gifts are just that….items which can be given. As I have been giving to you since I held you in my arms as an infant. When I could still see with human eyes what was before me.. I have had the confidence of gods, but it is your confidence I most desire. You are my daughter as much as Oedipus's."

"My family is cursed. The House of Atreus is a tragic one."

"But out of all tragedy springs joy. Look how the winter kills the blossoms, yet from their death they spring up again when the seasons turn. Your child will be that joy!"

"You said my child would be raised in the land of death."

"In the land of death…not the state of death. Hades will fly with him on the dragon to show him the universe. He will be cherished, coming from a deep love, as no child has. Your father and mother will know him."

"It will be a boy…." Ismene let this sink in. Her mind envisioned a small boy with skin like polished silver and the darkest night coloring his hair and eyes.

"You are the last sacrifice your household must make," Tieresias said.

"And the gods will be satisfied that the house of Atreus has paid its price for such happiness of a little child. I do not believe it."

"You must. I have many things yet to teach you…."

But then he fell silent. They watched the great eagle trace circles above them.

"Why did you beat me when I killed the bird?"

"So you would remember never to kill another. And have you?"

"No, of course not…" she touched his shoulder. "But I have seen you sacrifice birds."

"In religious ceremony. Not for sport. It was the only bad thing you ever did."

Her head rested on his bony shoulder.

"I do not want to kill birds now even for religious ceremony. Perhaps you taught me too well."

"Perhaps I did. I should have known Oedipus would not discipline you. He killed the man who was his father many years before….and vowed never to kill again."

"Or hurt?"

"Or hurt."

A peace came over them as they watched the tireless eagle. Ismene smiled.

"My father was the sweetest man I knew…," she whispered.

"Did you enjoy seeing him in the land of death?"

"No. They went through motions as though in a dance, but they did not seem alive…." As an afterthought she said, "As it must be with dead people."

"And sometimes with the living. But not with you, Ismene. You do not make motions."

"Do you love me so much, Tieresias?"

"As my life," he said, and they both fell quiet, letting the wind talk for them.

* * *

The next few weeks were peaceful weeks. Creon was out of the kingdom, and his minister, Hectar, did not trouble Ismene. She wondered if he knew she had even returned. Those who had made their way to Tieresias's eyrie seemed fiercely loyal to her family, when they spoke to her at all. She hoped the world might forget the House of Atreus and allow her baby to be born here, where Tieresias could befriend her.

Tieresias soon dissuaded her of this wish. One night, when the cloak of purple spread across the heavens, he took her out to watch the advent of the stars.

"Creon has learned of your presence....once again, you must flee."

Where do I go now? She thought briefly, regretfully, of Hades.

"The journey will be easier this time. Creon is in the middle of a war. I can handle the assassin he sends, but he will not stop trying for your death. Especially now that he knows you are with child."

"Where do you send me?" again she asked the question.

"To Hippolyta, Queen of the Amazons."

"Hippolyta ! The wild Amazon queen who tamed Theseus? Why may I not return to the netherworld?"

"Perserphone has heard of you. You do not want to incur her jealousy...."

Ismene moved in surprise. "Jealousy? She hardly gave Hades a thought. He was thought by her to be her tormentor, not her lover."

Tieresias laughed, "There is nothing like the attentions of another woman to make a wife think of what she may have lost."

"Does she know I will bear Hades's child?"

"No. But she knows you took his heart away when you left...."

"Then where is this heart? I see no heart...." Ismene held out her hands. "If I took his heart, I left him mine."

"Child, this is not a question of hearts. It is a question of safety. Hippolyta and her band of women warriors have vowed to protect all females in need. I lived with them once, when I was..." Tieresias cleared his throat. "I was a woman who needed them. And they not only sheltered me, but they shared all their adventures with me. There are worse places you could go."

"Tell me about your life...."

"Not tonight. The light will smear across the sky before I am done relating my childhood. A longer, colder night is the night for such a story...."

"Then, tell me how you came to lose your sight."

"It happened after I was changed into a man by Hera. She transformed me from a young woman into the most arrogant of men.

I thought my rights the most important rights. Once, when visiting Olympus, I caught the eye of Athena at a banquet. That night, I went to her chamber, believing she desired me...."

"Athena is a virgin goddess."

"Yes. But I did not know her virginity was of choice. I thought she had never met the man to whom to give her maidenhead...I came upon her in the bath. Hera had me followed, believing, rightly, I was up to no good. The glorious goddess was just emerging when I came upon her. I forgot that as a mortal I had no right to look upon a nude deity. Not in the flesh. Immediately, Hera went to Zeus, who threw a thunderbolt, blinding me forever. Then Zeus hurled me from the edge of Olympus. I never returned until Hades needed someone to defend him for defiling a maiden. You know that story! I pleaded his case as best I could. He wept and stormed outside the circle of decision."

"I want to hear no more about Hades's marriage!" Ismene cried.

"It is part of the legends that men sing at the fire. You will hear it everywhere."

"It is not the whole of his legend. I am the part which will remain unsung."

Tieresias laughed. "You have gone from being a righteous maiden to becoming a jealous woman."

Ismene had to laugh as well. "Yes, I am a jealous woman. But you are accurate that I need to escape Creon. Once more, flight. I was enjoying our time together...."

Tieresias drew her close in embrace. "We will be together again. After Creon's death...for he will die."

"And who will be the next king?"

"I have not yet looked in to that mystery," Tieresias answered primly.

Ismene knew that when his voice took on that tone, she must not question further. She snuggled closer in his bony grip. "When do I leave?"

"Tomorrow. I am sending the child, Xerxes, with you...."

"A boy? Will the Amazons accept a male child?"

"If he comes with you. He needs a mother...."

"I should think he will have several there."

"They do not nurture any but their own. Just as with the animals..."

Ismene remembered a lion cub from her youth that mistook a sheep for his mother. The sheep, filled with the milk for her own lambs, did let him feed from her breast. Tieresias had said such "mistakes" happen rarely.

"How will we find our way?"

"I will give half the map to you and half to Xerxes. Together, you will know the path. It is a long path. Now you need to rest...."

"How can I give you up again?" Ismene cried, her fingers digging into his arm. She thought the prophet looked older, his very skin seemed ready to blow away like the sands in the wind. She never knew how old he really was. Eurydice told her once that Tieresias was there before the city was built. Creon's grandfather remembered the seer. He was a force that moved easily between gods and mankind. In spite of his invincibility, she feared his death.

"You will see me again....and Hades..." His fingers stroked her into weariness. "Oh child, there is no end to what you will see! Even, like myself, when you see no more!"

* * *

Xerxes was standing over her when she awoke.

"I am here with food, and with your bundle to take," he announced.

"And Tieresias?"

"He is preparing potions for us."

Xerxes smiled a fierce smile.

Ismene looked at the sky. The sun disc of the god Apollo was already hung high in the heavens. Her gaze returned to Xerxes, examining him carefully for the first time.

"You know we are to make a journey together?"

"I am prepared to protect you, Princess." He drew back his shoulders, standing tall. Her smile was immediate. This boy with uncombed hair, and rags had a nobility in him.

"Thank you for your protection, and I hope you will also provide me with good company...."

Tieresias appeared behind Xerxes, his face serious.

"You must move more quickly now. Creon's men are coming up the hillside."

"How shall I escape them?"

"Xerxes will take you to a secret chamber in my cave."

She tried to remember what chamber this could be, as Xerxes pulled her quickly by the hand. She thought Tieresias had shown her all the secrets of his eyrie. The rock that hid the entrance was not easily pushed aside. It took the strength of woman and boy to open the shaft. Once inside, it took all their strength to roll the stone back.

Her eyes adjusting, Ismene saw this chamber as a match for the many mirrored chamber in the Netherworld where Hades looked at the living. For a moment, she hoped to see the form of the god of death on the shiny walls. His image was strong inside her as was his expected child. Her physical body was wrapped in his great robe. Tieresias must come here when she was asleep to look with his inner eyes onto other worlds.

"*When did you learn of this place?*" she whispered to Xerxes.

"Tieresias hid me here from my father when he came roaring drunk to find me some moons ago....he told me no one could ever hurt me. This room is protected by more than its location. It is protected by Zeus himself, who blessed it."

"I know another room like this...." Ismene took Xerxes hand in hers. "And I wonder if there are more than the two we share..."

On the walls, began to appear the faces she had seen on statues of the gods and goddesses of Mount Olympus. She saw them move around the throne room of mighty Zeus, talking as the courtiers of the Theban palace conversed. Demeter whom she had met on the riverbank of the Styx stood by herself. This meant that Perserphone was in residence in the Netherworld! Tieresias had said as much. The visual of a lonely parent made the moment real to Ismene. Quickly, she pulled her eyes away from Demeter to see the interplay between Aphrodite and Ares, two guilty lovers. Their fingers brushed in passage as they moved among the others. Aphrodite's gnarled husband, Haesphaetus, frowned suddenly, then smiled as his wife leaned her body towards him.

"Who are these people?" demanded Xerxes.

"These are not people. Not mortals. They are the masters, and we are their puppets," Ismene spoke gently. "You are seeing Olympus itself, and the deities that we worship as stone figures in the temples have come alive."

"How can they be gods when they are so foolish?"

"It is why we are foolish, being made in their images."

A sudden movement in Ismene's stomach reminded her she would bear the results of her own foolishness. Then she remembered her son would grow up without her care, the way Xerxes grew without the ministrations of his mother.

"Do you feel unwell, princess?" Xerxes was instantly solicitous when he saw Ismene's face go pale with pain.

"No. It is one of the small pains I will have over the next few moons. I am with child, Xerxes," Ismene explained gently.

"Oh…" His puzzlement was evident. She laughed. He was very young, despite his attempts at gallantry.

"Women bear children all the time. Even those who toil in the fields or fight their enemies…even the Amazons. I know that your mother died giving birth to you. But I will not die. It has been foreseen that this child will be born."

"And was it foreseen that you will live through it?"

"Yes." She took his small strong hands in hers. "Yes, I will not die from this child. There are other events in my future."

"Then we must flee. Tieresias says your danger is great."

"I will not leave until that old bird, himself, bids me farewell. He is now the most important person in my life." She let go of his hands. Hades's robe slipped from her shoulders. The sudden chill of the cave overcame her. Quickly, Xerxes ran forward and retrieved the fallen garment, placing it again on her shoulders.

"I know Tieresias cares for you. He told me you were his real daughter. Your father dedicated you to the path when you were born. Tieresias says you even looked different than your sister and brothers."

"Yes, I resemble my mother. She, too, has the yellow hair and blue eyes. And she also was surprised that no other child except myself had those looks. Sometimes, my father teased her saying that Apollo, god of the sun, was her lover in his place."

When she was very small, Ismene had envied Antigone's olive skin and brown eyes. She used to love to braid her older sister's hair, which had the color of the rich earth. Later, Tieresias told Ismene that every flower has its own beauty.

Ismene began to forget despising her own looks.

"I look like my father," Xerxes sighed. Ismene examined his face, which seemed old before its time. It was not a soft face, but blunted around the jaw and mouth. "I don't have the look of a seer."

"Does Tieresias say you are a seer?"

"He says I will know seers. How do you know seers unless you can see yourself?"

"I think he means you will understand the seeing, but you will not be able to see."

"I don't understand that."

Ismene laughed, "I don't think Tieresias always understands himself when he says something. It is as though someone else were speaking from inside him the way..." She remembered the Oracle at Delphi. "He is the instrument for the sound, much like the flute plays a melody. Break the flute open, you will not find that melody. And yet..."

"It sounds." Xerxes smiled at her. "I think we will be good friends."

"Better friends than enemies..." Tieresias's voice came from the entrance to the room.

"Are the soldiers..."

"They have gone their way, Ismene. I sent them on a false path after I convinced them with much hocus-pocus that I could see in the flame where you were hiding?"

"And where am I supposed to be hiding?"

"In the ruins of Troy. Just the opposite way from where you will go."

"And they won't be angry with you for this lie?"

"Who says it is a lie? They will see a shade that will look like you ahead of them, always ahead. Their chase will come to nothing. Creon will not be pleased." He put his clawlike hand on her head. "And now, we will say farewell again...."

"I wanted you to be present at my child's birth."

"I will sense it on the walls of this room....and I will spill wine for your child's health and happiness."

Ismene took his face between her hands. "Can you follow us with images on this wall?"

"I cannot see...," Tieresias smiled. "This room has been dark to me for many years. I must go by intuition here. Although lately, I have asked Xerxes to describe..."

"I forget sometimes that you are blind."

"Yes, so did the soldiers. They believed what I said about looking into the fire and finding your image."

"You are really just a conjurer, like the man that came through with the jugglers and dancers."

"If you wish to describe me as such."

"Why do you keep this room?"

"For the one who will follow me."

She leaned forward and kissed him lightly on the lips. "No one can follow you."

He handed her the lambskin with a map drawn. It was in two pieces. Xerxes took one from her.

"You will need to leave by this cave...." Xerxes pulled her hand impatiently.

"Tieresias..."

"Yes, Ismene. I will let Hades know of his child. And your safety..."

The mention of Hades filled the emptiness within her. She thought of the god's frantic tongue on her body. Inside, the child was growing, bonding her to this deity forever.

Xerxes pulled her along the dark passage.

"How do you know of this escape?" she demanded.

"Tieresias put it on the map...."

"Ah, you have the first half..."

How many times must she propel through darkness, escaping what life would give to her? She felt a cold wind, and then they were outside, some distance from the craggy rocks where she saw a lone figure bent on the weight of a stick.

"Goodbye, old bird. Do not fly off to other kingdoms. I am coming back to you," she promised.

* * *

Xerxes was an excellent map reader. He guided her quickly around the city of Thebes through well-worn gullies. There was one moment of despair as she looked at the great Temple high on the hill, remembering her first happy years with her family.

"Do not regret!" she heard Tieresias's voice in her memory. He told her that it was not wise to think on the past.

"And yet the past is the most real thing to us...," she had argued.

"You may remember, but you must never regret the choices you took or how the fates wove that past into the fabric of your tapestry."

Xerxes began to sing when he felt they were safe from earshot of the soldiers who guarded the city. His voice was pure and thin like the little birds of morning. She smiled at him, thinking she knew why Tieresias loved the boy.

By the time the chariot of Apollo had sped through the arc of day they both were ready to sit by a clear spring and share bread and lentils.

"Tell me about my mother," Xerxes demanded. "You said you knew her."

"I was younger. But she was someone I could not forget. She sold my mother feathers from birds such as we have never seen here. Her

name was Adrianna....she seemed almost like a bird, herself..."
Ismene stopped herself before she could add, "As you do."

"My father says she was a whore he brought back from the wars."

"Your father has no understanding of beauty....or what can happen to a bird when it is caged."

"Are all men so stupid? I do not want to be a stupid man...."

"No. My father was not stupid. He was hotheaded when he was young, but he learned to temper his flame. Tieresias is not foolish...."

"But then Tieresias was not always a man," Xerxes said.

"You know that?"

"Everyone knows. They think he has some magic in him that can make him what he wishes. They fear crossing him. He might turn into a dragon!"

Ismene laughed outright. "I have met a dragon that was not so fearful."

She thought of her day with Hades in flight to the ends of the universe. How he stroked his dragon and slept against that scaly body while she ran through the shoreline of scarlet waters and blue sands.

"How do you know he wasn't fearful?"

"I rode on his back. He flew through the air."

"Will I ride on him?"

The smells of Hades suddenly emanated from his robe that she wore. "I do not know, Xerxes. The dragon does not live in this world." His expression grew puzzled. "I was in hiding. Tieresias made his magic for me to go to a place where the living do not go, where I met a god...," her voice trailed off.

"I don't suppose the amazons will have a dragon."

"I don't suppose," she agreed. "But now, we must look for shelter for the night. Wild beasts populate this world."

* * *

They found their shelter in a crumbling temple, long abandoned. It was a temple to Artemis. The population must have moved in closer to the city in the time of the last wars. Both of them curled under the altar, too tired to give the goddess her rites before they drifted into sleep.

As often in her dreams, Ismene was visited by figures that seemed as real to her as those she met while awake. Tonight, it was Artemis in whose temple she found refuge. She recognized the goddess from her many breasts filled with milk, her slanted cat eyes, and the procession of small animals following after.

"Dear goddess…" Ismene's dream-self rose to greet the divine form.

"Rest, Ismene. I have followed your journey on my cave wall….oh yes, I too have a cave that shows me the world outside." The voice of the goddess was low and full of the breath of winds. "You have always been a favorite of mine."

"I have worshiped at your altar."

"Yes, yes. Tieresias brought you to my temple as a very young girl. Tieresias loves you, which inclines me to love you. He and I…" Artemis stopped. In the moonlight, her smile lit the temple. "Tieresias stayed with me for a month on that island where Hades ravished his wife. It might be said I was ravished, too….more willingly; by Tieresias. He was handsome then. He came over the seas with Ulysses. And when he saw me there in the spring that bubbled out of the green earth, he bade Ulysses farewell. One drink of that water gave him eyes beyond his mortal eyes to see into the heart of a goddess. Before then I was a virgin, much like my sister, Athena."

"It was Athena who lost him his eyes."

"Or the remembrance of myself in her." Artemis's own golden eyes flashed. "Because he had been a woman he knew where my pleasures sat."

"But you let him leave you!" Ismene cried.

"We gods and goddesses cannot stay in this world of mortals too long. Our strength ebbs away. You want too much of us….and you rob us, even lovingly, of our immortality. Several times, I visited Tieresias in dreams as I am visiting you now to tell him there is one who watches over him….and now over you."

Ismene moved closer to this fecund goddess. Several animals rubbed against her ankles as she approached.

"I need your protection for this journey."

"Yes." Artemis ran her tongue over her lips. "Hades cannot help you here."

"Hades?"

"You are in my territory. Zeus would not let him help you. I know you carry his child. All of Olympus knows. We are pleased. Hades is a special favorite of mine. As a young god, he used to take me for rides on a great dragon...."

Ismene smiled, remembering such a dragon and such a ride.

"He is a different sort of god than his brothers," Artemis continued. "My father, Zeus, punishes without thought. My uncle, Poseidon, rides on the waves of his watery kingdom with an eye for tricking the sailors. All the victims of their angers end in the world of Hades, where he must take them in and soothe them down for eternity. His one violence was against Demeter's daughter, and he righted it by marrying her. Even then, the residents of Olympus shunned him...."

The two fell silent, their minds caught at the thought of Hades's loneliness.

"And now, he will have a son to love him," Ismene said at last.

"If you live..." Artemis licked her lips in a wolfish anxiety. "You still could be in great danger. Your uncle has fixed all his hatred upon you....and his anger is almost as mighty as my father's. Tieresias was right to send you into this wood. I am the goddess of all who wander outside the laws of the city. And the little boy who joins you..."

"He is in danger as well! Just by accompanying me."

"Xerxes will live his entire life in danger of one thing or another. Danger will be his teacher. He has a longer journey to make than even you, Ismene."

Ismene could see the outline of Artemis start to shimmer.

"Dear goddess, what did you come to tell me?"

"That I am with you as far as the sea. Then you are in my uncle's territory...."

"I cannot abide the water. I fear it."

"You crossed the waters of the Styx to find the Netherworld."

"Yes, it was important to outrun Creon's soldiers."

"It is still important...." Artemis was no more than a cloud with silver edges. "Go back to your body now. Sleep quietly....as you leave tomorrow, place flowers on this altar. Then I will know you have remembered my words."

Behind Artemis appeared a shadowy form with many mouths, eyes and arms that undulated into the darkness. Ismene knew the form was the god Morpheus who came to carry her dream-shape back to the vessel of her body. The eyes looked every way for possible intrusions while the arms gently lifted her spirit up into darkest regions. The next moment, Ismene was stung by the bright sunshine into waking. Xerxes was placing the last of the bread before her.

"You were smiling," he said, sitting cross-legged beside her.

"I had a visitor in the night. The goddess who is blessed in this temple came to me. Artemis. Deeply loved by Tieresias. She will protect us to the water. Then we are in danger of Poseidon."

Ismene rose, having finished the small amount of bread.

"Can you pick some flowers for me to leave for our protectress?"

Xerxes nodded, running off.

Immediately Ismene went from the temple's protection into the woods beyond to relieve herself in the comfort of the morning. The birds were singing from the temple's roof. Xerxes returned quickly with blossoms as red as blood intermingled with deep yellow flowers.

"Oh yes," Ismene thought, taking the bouquet. "You know how to please a goddess, young man."

"We should be gone. To linger is pleasant, but I do not trust a world at peace," Xerxes urged.

"Nor I," Ismene agreed, shaking out Hades's robe and folding it. She thought of the feral goddess. She would rather live under the care of Artemis than beg the ministrations of Hipployta, but Tieresias had willed it otherwise. Xerxes's eyes were patiently searching hers for clues as to how to proceed. Ismene would have to remind herself he was still a child, of whom Artemis had said he would live his entire life in danger.

"Danger will be your teacher, Xerxes," Ismene arranged the flowers on the altar as she spoke. "Artemis spoke of you last night. You, too, will have many an adventure in this life. It will keep your eyes open."

* * *

The day's journey took them through thick growths of trees and vines. At the end of the day they saw the sea and the beach leading to it through the upheld arms of trees. Both of them very hungry.

"I saw no animals to kill," Xerxes commented in apology.

"I saw no fruits growing. Artemis promised to protect us. I hope we have not displeased her." Ismene sank to the ground.

"I will go ahead to the great waters. Perhaps I can spear a fish...."

"No, Xerxes!" She felt fear filling up her veins. "Poseidon is a moody god. He has been known to trick humans into the deep waters where they drown."

"Look at your map, Princess. Mine is at an end here."

Her portion of the map, surprisingly enough, revealed nothing but water with a small dot of an island in the far corner marked as the land of the Amazons.

"We must go across this water, Xerxes," she said at last. "I do not know how, but we must find a way." An image of the flying dragon of Hades went through her like a shiver.

Xerxes stared intently at the piece of skin with the drawing on it.

"Princess..." he began, and then he shrugged, defeated by the thought.

She felt more tired than she had ever felt, her limbs dropping like a dying flower. The hunger and the barrier of the water pushed away her ability to think.

"We will rest here. In the woods where Artemis still rules. Tomorrow we will find food and hope...." She was unconvinced, yet she knew she must convince him. He had to be her strength now, young and unformed as he was.

He took the robe from her and unfolded it, covering her with the warmth of the full spread. The smells of Hades that clung to the robe soothed her. She managed to return a small smile.

"Come under the robe with me. We can share its warmth...."

"No, Princess. I will look for wood with which to make a fire."

"How will you start such a fire?"

Her question brought color to his cheeks. "I have been alone many times. Tieresias gave me a stone I can strike...."

"A fire would be good, Xerxes." She was beginning to take on a second energy. "We might find some bird eggs in that nest up there." In the twilight, she saw a large nest tottering on a small branch. If we had a fire, we might fetch some water...and cook the eggs."

They looked around for something to hold the water. Their voices took on a speed. The light was dying fast. She remembered the shade of Umbra, appearing prim and unhappy with the gifts of Hades to fill a mortal stomach. Shadows here were moving as though in a dance. One detached from the others, carrying a clay jug of water.

"From Artemis..." it whispered, identical to the voice of the rising breeze. "And the bird eggs. The boy is too tired to climb."

Another shadow moved behind the first. "And here is wood. The fire will help to keep the wild animals away...."

Both took a long drink from the clear water before they began to arrange the sticks. The stone Xerxes drew from beneath his robes looked humbled enough, but when he struck it on another stone two or three times a spark fell from it. The eggs, when boiled in the water, tasted more delicious to her than any food at any palace feast. The robe clung to her like the hungry arms of Hades during their one night of passion. As she fell asleep against the softness of a mossy outgrowth, she heard the voice of Artemis, "It was your choice to trust me, to stay here tonight. It was your doing, Ismene. We always have choices in our destiny."

* * *

In the night, it seemed she awoke and walked to the very edge of the woodland. The ground moved beneath her feet to help her legs find their strength. At the edge, she looked out to the great sea, watching Poseidon driving his chariot , pulled by sea serpents. He looked her way and raised his trident in acknowledgment. His expectant expression told her she was known to him.

"I carry your brother's child," she called to him, but the mouth of the wind opened and swallowed up her sound.

Then looking up in the sky, she saw Artemis's face appear in half. "We always have choices in our destiny." Ismene mouthed the words she heard Artemis say. Inside her, the child moved as though riding the wave along with the sea-god. Inside her, she knew there was a little sea, buoying him up and pushing him down. She was his lifeline. He would drown without her there in the womb.

* * *

When she woke, Xerxes was sitting beside her, his face set in a wide smile.

"A good sleep?" she questioned.

"Food. You must be special to the goddess…." He gestured, and she saw wrappings of grape leaves and a small skin of wine. A familiar scent hung in the air.

"Not to a goddess, but to a god I am special," she whispered. They ate heartily and washed in the stream that suddenly bubbled out of the earth. Ismene bit back tears that Hades had not shaken her from her slumber. Or had he sent Umbra? Here in the woods, it seemed as though the world flourished, but perhaps outside Demeter was starting to mourn, denying the earth its glory. That could mean only one thing, Perserphone was in the Netherworld. Hades could not come, himself, on his dragon to help her. Was Neptune saluting her with his trident or the servant of Hades that stood behind Ismene at the edge of those dark woods last night?

"And now, Princess." Xerxes's voice pulled her from her reverie. "We must think how to reach that world of the Amazons. Your map shows only water. It is too far for swimming. We must find another pathway over the waves."

Ismene could not see how they would build a boat between them. They lacked both tools and knowledge. And yes, the dark hand was pulling at her fear of the water itself. She heard Creon's angry voice in her head, "I will drown you...."

"I am defeated," she said at last. The boy's eyes met hers. His look told her he would not be defeated.

"There is a way through this." He shook his head. "I do not believe Tieresias would give us a task he believed was impossible."

"Not impossible for him. But for us..."

She thought of Artemis's vow of protection only until the couple reached the shoreline.

"I will go and swim in this water. Then I will understand the nature of this obstacle." Xerxes stepped out from the edge of the woodlands.

"Can you swim?"

"What can there be to swimming?"

"Exactly," Ismene laughed suddenly. "What can there be to breathing? To walking? To swimming? To drowning?"

Xerxes was puzzled, "You think I will drown."

"No, Xerxes. Drowning is my fear...." She touched his cheek reassuringly. "Ever since I was a small child. I saw a servant drown in the river trying to save his master. The loss of his life was the seed of fear that has grown ever since. Is there nothing you fear?"

"I don't fear drowning. It is my father I fear, when he is drunk...."

Ismene thought of Hades and the smell of his fear that rose up when he mentioned Perserphone. *Was it a fear of her loss? Or a fear of her? Of her unloving heart every time he reached for her?*

"And so," she sighed, "we all have our fears that defeat us in the most amazing of adventures." Maybe that was why Tieresias sent her to this place, to face that fear. She looked at the calm of the water, remembering how on that day at the edge of the universe she walked in a sea. Her fear was gone under the gaze of Hades.

"We will try this sea together." She pushed back her shoulders in determination.

"I should try first. My fear is not as great." Xerxes steadied her with his hand. Nevertheless, they walked together out of the dense woodland onto the white beach. The air was chilled, but the sunshine made the waters glow. She had Hades robe around her shoulders, emitting perfumes from plants that grew on the side of the Styx. She wanted to be worthy of bearing the son of a god. She would not retreat now.

The water moved between her toes. She would have gasped at its pull, except that Xerxes gasped before she could let out a sound.

"This water wants us," he declared. "But how does it want us. Is it a want that will aid us or kill us?"

They tried to move along the shore, but the water was adamant.

"My sea is not friendly to you," spoke a deep voice behind them. Turning at the same moment, they saw Poseidon sitting on a single wave.

"Why is your sea angry with us?" demanded Ismene. "We have not hurt you or your subjects."

"Mortals should not beckon to the waters. Mortals belong on the land," Poseidon boomed.

"But it is land we seek. The island over there." Ismene pointed to a distant spot of green.

"Those foolish women? What does the daughter of Oedipus have to do with such females?" Poseidon laughed, causing more waves to rise.

"We were instructed to hide there until the Princess has her child," Xerxes blurted out before Ismene could silence him.

"Oh yes..." Poseidon slid his sea-green eyes over Ismene's swelling body. "I have heard the gossip in Olympus. My younger brother has taken his hospitality too far once again. He was always an excessive young fellow."

"Do not count me as a victim. I bear his child with pride. It is not for that reason Tieresias sends us to the Amazons."

"I have a quarrel with Tieresias. He is careful never to walk too close to my kingdom's boundaries." Poseidon spat out a great wave.

Ismene was silent, letting the anger break upon the shoreline. Tieresias had a background with the gods that he only hinted at in his memories for her. She did not think it prudent to question why Poseidon was angry with him. The calm waters might be needed for her to cross safely with Xerxes. Instead she smiled:

"I am not sure Tieresias is sending me to safety. He has left us here with no way across your world."

Poseidon leaned on his trident, searching her face for a reason behind her smile, "Why is my brother not here, pleading your case for you?"

Why, indeed! She wished she knew. Hades had told her he loved her but did not bid her farewell after their night of lovemaking nor come to her even as a dream. Did he not desire this child within her? Or was he too frightened of Perserphone's wrath should he intervene on Ismene's behalf?

"I am capable of pleading my own case," she spoke defiantly. "I learned my worth from my parents. It is a weak mortal who needs the intervention of a god."

"It is a proud mortal who thinks she can argue her case without the backing of a deity," Poseidon reprimanded her. Then he shrugged, the waters rolling off his scaly back. "I will let you pass. It will be my pleasure. It may even annoy that rascal brother of mine who will not show his face in the light of day to protect his unborn child. However, I will warn you about the Amazon women. They are hardest of their own sex. Show them no weakness….and guard the boy by your side."

Xerxes stepped in front of her, "I need no protection from a pregnant woman."

Poseidon shook his fish-scaled head from side to side, "You have much to learn about the world, my boy. Should you not be cautious you will soon be reminiscing about this fair princess with Hades in his kingdom."

"We must make our farewells to Artemis," Ismene prompted.

"Be quick! I have waters more vast than this to patrol." Poseidon shook a wary finger.

Ismene knelt upon the ground, conjuring the image of Artemis in her mind. The goddess appeared there with her court of animals, smiling.

"Goddess," Ismene spoke aloud. "I humble myself in gratitude for your kindnesses. Please allow me to look upon you when I return to this woodland."

Xerxes pulled her to her feet, whispering, "*I do not trust this Water god. He may change his mind at any moment.*"

Poseidon was, indeed, scowling where a smile had been.

"We are ready," Ismene spoke over the crashing of a thousand small waves upon the shore. A storm was appearing in Poseidon's palm which he seemed prepared to hurl.

"Climb upon my other hand," Poseidon commanded, increasing his already great size as he spoke until he grew into the clouds.

Ismene and Xerxes scrambled upon the Water god's scaly palm. Thus Poseidon stood, the storm in one hand and the travelers in the other.

"I will set this storm down to confuse Creon's men who are following you," Poseidon explained.

"I did not know they were so close!" Ismene cried.

"Then you don't know your uncle. He is determined to close your life before another can be born to the house of Atreus...," Poseidon spoke with urgency. His right hand threw the compacted storm which scattered over the edge of the sea. His other hand let Xerxes and Ismene gently down on the beach of a small island, far from the concert of lightening and thunder.

"I had heard you were a trickster god," Ismene said, sitting in the sand.

"I am a trickster god." Poseidon shrunk again to his original size. His sea-green eyes overflowed with briny tears. "It is my shame."

"But you are kind to us," Xerxes protested.

"To play a trick on someone else. Creon, who has never honored me with proper rites, although he has used my seas to sail his armies for conquering."

"I give you honor now." Ismene came to the shoreline, touching the water with her fingers.

Poseidon waved his trident which had been floating on the surface of the sea. As quickly as he had come, he was gone. Only a wreath of seaweed floated where he had previously been seen.

"And I suppose now we must look for the Amazons...," Xerxes sighed.

"No," declared a voice, as sweet as the ring of a deep bell, "They have found you already. With all that racket from Poseidon, how could they not be drawn to the shore."

Turning, Ismene saw a woman; dressed in the furs of animals, one breast gone, holding a bow and arrow. The woman's hair was red as though she carried a searing fire on her head. Behind the woman at a distance stood several other women , one-breasted and clad in fur, but lacking the fiery crimson of the speaker's hair.

"Are you Hippolyta?" Ismene extended her hand to the strange woman.

"You know that I am." The woman's grip on her hand was strong.

"Tieresias sends his greetings and asks that you shelter us in the name of his long friendship with you."

"Long friendship?" The woman threw back her head, laughing. "That rascal took advantage of half the women in my tribe. He, or she—whichever the scamp chooses to become—had them sighing so deep with love they were not good for battle. It was then Theseus attacked us. I was forced to marry the headstrong man just to ransom my country. After which..." a smile formed on Hippolyta's lips, "I left him in a state of defeat, sighing with love for me. I took my women back to this world and made them understand Tieresias was never coming back. For the time I gave them to recover, they wrote down the poems of our people and found silly men we keep for breeding purposes. Tieresias gave his word he would never come to this island again."

"Will you shelter us?" Xerxes wanted a definite answer.

"You are too young for breeding. Why are you here, my lad?"

"Tieresias insisted he come with me." Ismene put her arm around Xerxes's shoulder protectively.

"Is he your son?"

"No, I could never have borne a child this old. What are you thinking?" laughed Ismene. "He is my friend."

"And that roundness of your belly?"

"That is my son who will be. Tieresias hoped I could have the child here under your protection."

"What is special about this child?" Hippolyta moved closer. Her eyes caught attention to Hades's robe which blew in the wind behind Ismene. "You are the one. I have heard the whispers from zephyr to zephyr about the cursed daughter of Oedipus who won the heart of the god of death."

"I need a place of safety…."

Hippolyta's gray eyes narrowed, "Why does Hades not help you?"

"I left quickly. Tieresias summoned me back."

Hippolyta licked her blood-red lips with anticipation, "Does Perserphone know?"

"If you say even the breezes are gossiping, she must have heard as well," Ismene responded, wondering how Hades's wife would feel about the possibility of another woman bearing the god a child.

"She can be difficult. I told her mother to leave her with us. She was a spoiled child. The daughter of a goddess, beautiful to the eye….but so selfish! We might have trained her mind to look outside herself. I heard Hades was always at his wit's end on how to amuse her. She felt no obligation to amuse him."

Ismene remembered Hades's few words about the frigidity of his wife towards him. Was Perserphone as chilly towards everyone else? Her only sight was of a lovely young woman hurrying to her mother's arms as Ismene had anxiously run to the embrace of Jocasta.

Hippolyta came even closer, her face close to Ismene's.

"Are you happy to learn the faults of this wife?"

"No. I want Hades to be happy. Perhaps his son will make him so."

"You plan to return to Hades?"

In a rush came memories of that world beneath the one on which she walked. "I will reach Hades someday when my mission here is fulfilled."

"What mission is that? You come from a family cursed through all the ages."

"Tieresias plans something for me. Must a mission be pleasant? Mine will be what must be done. I lost all my beloved family, then my lover, and now I must bear a child only to forsake it." Ismene felt the tears fall, unbidden, from her eyes.

"Then it is our job to cheer you up!" Hippolyta slapped Ismene's shoulder with a hearty gesture. "And you, too, young fellow!" She poked Xerxes in the ribs.

Suddenly, Ismene liked Hippolyta very much. She went arm-in-arm to the great palace just beyond the beaches. The gates swung open, and wherever Ismene turned her eyes, women were at work, doing the labors of men. Xerxes received several curious stares. He ran to keep pace with the swift Hippolyta who, by now, was fairly dragging Ismene behind her.

"There is a poetess here who wrote some words that could be your words," Hippolyta smiled, "She wrote:

> *The way across the water*
> *is not as dangerous as the journey*
> *across the country of my Life.*
> *The boat I ride in*
> *may tip me into a bottomless sea,*
> *but my Life can toss me higher into sky*
> *than I can even measure.*

"And yet it is the water that I fear," Ismene replied. "I always have."

"The sea is not your friend. Poseidon let you come to us on a whim. Sometimes his whims go one way, sometimes another. By tomorrow, he may be plotting a spectacular storm to mar your return....he is not friendly with his brother, Hades."

"And is Zeus friendly with Hades?"

"Zeus cannot be friendly with any one. His court smells with the odor of plots and treachery. Even his wife, Hera, cannot know his thoughts. Hades was so much younger. Foolhardy."

"That is a different Hades than I know!" Ismene demurred.

"Zeus wore out his arm trying to beat sense into that young god. Finally, he sent him off to the Netherworld as an exile. Hera reminded her husband that Hades could set up court there. She had fancied the god herself and thought it would be convenient to meet him away from Olympus. But something happened to Hades when he was handed responsibility. He took it seriously. And so the two older brothers agreed that Hades should rule the Underground kingdom."

"How do you know all this?"

"Tieresias told me," Hippolyta grinned. "He was always good for gossip."

Ismene had never known Tieresias in any other manner than an old man of great wisdom who was blind and shriveled. She could only imagine the young Tieresias, who was female and male, moving between the gods and men with such ease that all who remembered him had strong thoughts about him.

Seeing the puzzlement on Ismene's face, Hippolyta sighed, "How do you think Tieresias found his wisdom? He did not just trip across it one day. He came to it through life, the way you will come to yours. And this young man to his. The way your child will find a path to follow. You are fearful of the water, but the sea we ride on is not just the sea that Poseidon rules. Perhaps your waters are different ones."

* * *

Xerxes was taken to the compound of the men. Hippolyta said it was for his protection. No woman would sleep tonight if the young man was kept at the palace.

"It is not our way. There were many reasons why we abandoned the world outside this island. We have all had mothers, sisters, friends, lovers who were abused at the hands of males. Some of us returned, finding the company of men necessary. We take the vows of the Warrior, and our breast is cut off as a pledge to that way of life. Of course, you do not look like much of a warrior to me...."

Ismene was growing dizzy from the wine Hippolyta had poured for her. The Amazon queen seemed to have great endurance for the strong drink.

"I am here to learn whatever you have to teach me," Ismene said at last. The musicians were playing softly now, after a wild, whirring song.

"I cannot teach anyone so sleepy. In the morning, I will show you our island. It is not so large. And you can visit Xerxes, so reassure yourself of his safety."

Ismene washed her body in a pool of water that was on the terrace adjoining her room. She examined her growing stomach. It was this moment when she missed her mother most. There were so many questions that could not be answered by others. How would the pain be? How long would it last? Did you love your baby when you first saw it? Did the child love you immediately?

Lying on the sleeping couch naked, she watched the careless dance of the bats in the night skies. She remembered her one night with Hades in the cave emptied of bats who flew up through an opening into this world.

"Tell him when you return into the earth that I miss him," she admonished the dark-winged creatures. "Tell him I hope Perserphone makes him feel the pleasure he gave to me. Tell him how much I love him...."

And with that last thought, she slipped into the arms of Morpheus, the god of sleep, who carried her off into the temporary kingdom of her dreams.

* * *

Tieresias visited her dreams that night, slow of gait, leaning on his twisted stick. He touched her into that waking within the sleeping. She gasped, her dream-self sitting up straight.

"Creon has imprisoned me," he said. She looked at his torn robes and the bruises about his sightless eyes.

"He would not dare!"

"He is accusing me of treason for harboring you. I am to be put on trial..."

"I must return to defend you."

"Defending me would seal my doom. I have the good will of many of the citizens, but if you return, he will say it proves his charge against me."

"I cannot leave you there in Creon's prison!" The passion of her voice shook even her slumbering body which moaned and tossed.

"I am in good company. The King of Corinth is here, too," Tieresias smiled.

"Xerxes shall return then. He will raise an army against…"

Tieresias frowned. "Have I taught you nothing? Xerxes is a boy. Someday, he will be a great leader. Today he sulks that he is separated from you. I came to tell you this in a dream, because I may not see you again on this earth."

"You cannot leave me! You are the one constant of my life!" Her dream-shape fell at the prophet's feet, hugging his knees tightly. "Everyone leaves me….."

"We all die alone. Even in company, we die alone," Tieresias shrugged, and then he put his clawlike hand against her hair. "But your child will be with you soon."

"And even that child must leave me."

"Yes." It was final. "Hades will take him when the time is right."

Ismene rose, her height equal to that of the Seer.

"I must know if you can bear the pain of the execution."

"There are drugs."

"Creon can be cruel. He will not bury you. You will be condemned to a death that is solitary. Hades cannot allow you into the Netherworld unless someone buries you…."

Tieresias held her in embrace." The birds will come, one by one, to drop a stone down. In time, I will be buried."

"Do you fear it? death?"

"Child, I have lived with fear every day since my birth. Fear will be an old friend to me by now. Death will be a new friend."

"How will I learn all I need to take your place in the eyrie?"

"You are wise even now. Even though you cling to me like a frightened child, scared of the storm that is mixing in the distance."

"But Creon will de defeated. He will die alone."

"And he will not have the birds…."

"Eurydice awaits him in the Kingdom of Death. For her sake, he must be honored with funeral rites…."

"Then make certain that he is." Tieresias leaned forward to kiss her brow. The kiss burned deeply into her skin. She was not ready to let him go.

"There is something in this blindness. My father only became wise when he lost his eyes…."

"You have need of your eyes. Both pairs." His voice was impatient.

"I still feel there is something I can do to save you from your fate.."

"No." His voice was harsh. "I run to this ending as a maiden to the festival."

His form was fading in her dream-grasp. She could feel the solid flesh changing into mist.

"I love you, Tieresias." She felt helpless as she spoke. Immediately, her dream-self pulled him to her, kissing his mouth, which hung in the center of the gossamer cloud. Almost the moment after she awoke, she threw on Hades's robe and ran to the entrance of her chamber.

"Where is Queen Hippolyta's sleeping quarters?" she demanded of a surly guard.

"The queen never wishes to be disturbed so late," the woman said, stamping her feet as though in protest to the question.

"I demand to know…," Ismene began, but was stopped by a touch on her shoulder. She turned to find Hippolyta.

"We respect the silence of the night," Hippolyta admonished her.

"I have a serious matter to discuss with you. Tieresias has been imprisoned."

"I will not ask how you came to know this thing," Hippolyta sighed. "Please tell me what you expect me to do?"

"You must send your army to free him, of course." Ismene wondered how a queen could be so stupid.

Hippolyta signaled the guard away.

"I send my army to battle only in the most serious of times."

"These times are serious!"

"Tieresias is an old man. Death would have come to him soon, only Creon brings it sooner."

"You protected him once," Ismene reminded her.

"It was not his time for death. Besides, then, he was a young woman with many allurements. Now, he has lived his life."

The clear, steady gaze of the Amazon queen told Ismene there was no argument she would accept. Ismene sunk back against the marble palace wall.

"I cannot save him," she spoke slowly, trying to accept the words she was speaking.

"You are tired," Hippolyta said at last." Tieresias should not have bothered you with his troubles."

"He did not come to bother me; he came to say goodbye." Ismene did not ask how Hippolyta knew it was Tieresias's image that came to her.

"And did you say goodbye to him?"

Ismene silently nodded.

"Then all is well." Hippolyta's voice was gentle as she placed her hand against Ismene's cheek. "You are fortunate to have the power to summon those you love in your dreams. Even for such sad leave-takings."

"Come and sit with me for a moment. I will make a potion to help you sleep without these dreams. Your child is the one you are to save now."

Ismene felt numb under the weight of her own helplessness. She followed Hippolyta into the chamber which glowed with a thousand lights.

"I am afraid of the dark," Hippolyta explained.

"And I, of the water," Ismene nodded. "Tieresias told me once he feared the flame."

"And yet these are elements of our life here on earth—darkness, water, and fire," Hippolyta remarked, pouring from a pitcher into a chalice.

"No more wine!" Ismene protested.

"This drink is made from herbs gathered near the compound where the men live. It is helpful in fertility….and then strong in the womb."

The taste ran through Ismene like a clear, deep stream. She drank as though her thirst could not be quenched.

"Now," Hippolyta led her to the terrace, "I will rock you in my arms. You will think of the child you carry, not of the prophet who has already lived more lives than you can guess."

Ismene felt the shelter of Hades's cloak. "I am not the least bit tired," she protested. The cloak felt heavy on her shoulders. Hippolyta put her arms around the young girl, drawing her in.

"It is a long time since I rocked someone in distress in my embrace." Hippolyta's voice skimmed over the night.

"Whom did you rock this way?" Ismene asked, her eyelids already heavy.

"Theseus, on our wedding night. He was weeping when he realized I did not love him. By the time he fell asleep, I was weeping as well. We awoke in the morning, made sweet love, and then I left him as he lay sated on the bed."

"You did not speak so well of Theseus earlier."

"I forgot until this moment the pleasure he gave me," Hippolyta drew in her breath. "He was a haughty king, but in our wedding chamber, he became like a child with a first wish."

"And still, you left him?"

"I had responsibilities," Hippolyta reminded her, "as do you. Why else would you have left Hades when Tieresias summoned you back?"

Ismene had no answer. Her mouth seemed filled with some sweet honey that ran into her throat and through her body. Maybe there was no answer. She never disobeyed Tieresias but that one time when she had killed a bird as a child. The pain was not just in the beating he gave her, but also in the betrayal of his trust.

* * *

She visited Xerxes the next day, guided by the surly guard from the evening before whose name was Livia. The day light seemed to improve Livia's disposition. A large woman with an unruly shock of hair pointing every which way, Livia's footsteps could easily be heard far off.

"Do these men ever come to the palace?" Ismene inquired by way of conversation as Livia stormed across the meadow.

"Only at certain moon times." Livia stopped abruptly as though walking and talking at the same time were beyond her capabilities. "We are not supposed to become fond of them. Some do."

"Do you?" Ismene saw Livia's mouth twitching as though she wished to say more.

"I did," Livia pulled the words from deep inside her. Her face turned a bright red. "He was a good man. Kind to the touch. Unlike the others. He never called me 'ugly'."

"Is he still here?"

"No, he was fed."

"You mean, he ate?"

"No, I mean, he was fed to the hundred-armed giant that comes this way on his journeys...."

"I thought there were no more giants."

"Some. They hide away from Zeus. When they are hungry they go in search of food. They travel under the storms that Poseidon creates. Zeus usually cannot follow their journeys from Olympus with the heavy clouds. One likes coming here. There are always a few men who have annoyed Queen Hippolyta. She solves the problem of the possible revolt as well as sending the giant on his way, well sated."

And this was the very queen who had rocked Ismene to sleep last night!

"Oh Livia, how awful that must have been for you. Did you have to watch?"

"She makes everyone watch. It's a festival day." Tears were running unchecked down Livia's face. "It was quick. The giant ate him first. The giant was starving by then."

"But what did your man do to displease her?"

"He asked to wed me and take me back to his country."

Impossible, of course. Hippolyta spoke of these men the way a farmer speaks of a bull. Their use was in mating, not in marrying.

"And do you not feel anger at your queen?"

"No." Livia looked around." That would be treason."

With this said, she started moving again, Ismene running fast to keep up with her. They passed over a hill and into a deep forest. The sea air filled Ismene's senses. She saw a long fence and a man walking before it. The man was dressed simply and unarmed. When he spied Livia, he began to wave. Livia lifted her hand in return.

"Is it time for the mating?" The man ran up to Livia, taking her hands in greeting.

"No. Certainly not. You are over anxious. You must learn to hide that face," Livia cautioned him, withdrawing her hands.

"I don't remember this lass," the man said, turning his attention to Ismene.

"She is a guest of the queen. Her traveling companion was left with you last night."

"That child? Why would someone bring a child here?"

"Xerxes is not my child," Ismene smiled. "He came to protect me. Tieresias wished it to be so."

"I do not know this Tieresias," the man said with a wrinkle of his nose, "but he must know the Amazons particularly dislike male children."

"Which is why he is being kept with you. Do not waste our time, Zeno. We know how unhappy you have been since the last mating. I would not talk about it so openly. The hunger of the giant can include your paltry frame," Livia warned.

Zeno hung his head as she scolded him. When her words were done, he lifted his face with a newfound smile.

"Oh Livia, you are not as fierce as you look!"

"Yes, I am. I have hardened my heart since…" Livia bit her lip and looked away. "And you should harden yours. Chloe is no different than a hundred other women put out to mate."

"No, Chloe is so especially unlike those hundred other women!" Zeno protested. As he spoke, he was leading them through the compound. Several young men looked up in interest at Ismene, noted her swollen stomach, and looked away. Ismene saw Xerxes straight ahead, practicing archery with five older men.

"Xerxes!" she called. At the sound of her voice, he dropped the bow and came running to her side, astonishing onlookers by hugging her hard.

"Are we leaving yet?" Xerxes asked anxiously.

"No, Xerxes. Are you unhappy here?"

"I thought I would be with you. That was the wish of Tieresias."

"It was not the wish of Queen Hippolyta," Livia interjected.

"I think you are safer here. And you will learn some skills that a young man should know in a dangerous world."

Xerxes looked at her questioningly. Then he turned his gaze to Livia. "You must watch over the Princess for me. I need your promise," he said.

"I will watch over myself, Xerxes," Ismene rebuked him gently.

"She is under the care of the queen. We are all watching over her," Livia spoke grudgingly.

"I have heard things about this queen," Xerxes whispered.

Ismene thought of Livia's story of feeding rebellious men to the hundred-handed giant. A giant that should no longer exist! In the War between the titans and the giants, before Zeus created mankind, the Titans had taken over the world. Tales of such giants were told to frighten children. Her nurse had told her such a story once when she wanted to keep Ismene from wandering off. The giant would get her! Eat her!

"The queen speaks to me kindly," Ismene replied quite honestly. And it would do no good to tell Xerxes of the dream about Tieresias's capture. His blood was already running hot with adventure.

"Come, Xerxes, we will let Livia show us this city of men. So different from that of the women at the center of the island." Ismene kept her voice light. Livia threw her a glance to show that Livia, at least, was not fooled.

The three walked, each within their thoughts, around the compound. Men were farming, but also men were sewing and cooking. In the other city women were doing the same tasks without sexual division. It seemed a sad world where the two sexes met only to copulate. Ismene remembered Hippolyta's soft words for the enemy, Theseus. Could such a woman come to love this man? Could these men and women, separated by so much mistrust, learn to live together? Livia had not gone against her queen for love, even to watch him fed to the giant. Whatever Ismene would learn here must be a positive lesson.

As they walked, Livia started singing in her deep voice. In a second, Xerxes joined her in the song that Ismene remembered from her nurse's ministrations at bedtime:

Come part the waves
And split the heart
Of mountains.
Bring me home
To where
There is no care
But the doves cooing
Their gently worry.
I have traveled
Many years
To find the journey out
Was also
The return.

The baby moved inside her, and her hand went in wonder to her stomach.

"My poor little one, you will soon be learning the pathways of the heart," she thought. She pinched back her tears. This child would grow and wonder others. Not herself. "What can I give you but a safe womb in which to wait for the flood ways to open…?"

* * *

That night, she sat with Hippolyta at the court drinking the heavy wine and asking, "Why must the men be kept apart?"

"Men cannot be trusted. They are too impulsive. Some of them have risen up against me in the past."

"Maybe they would not rise up if they were included."

Hippolyta's eyes narrowed, "Have you learned nothing from your own life? Look at your brothers and the ruin they brought on themselves through their impetuous desire to rule. Look at your own father who killed his father in a fit of rage. Men are greedy for the whole universe. And when they obtain it, they will not share it."

Ismene fell silent for a moment, then replied, "You are seeing half of the whole man. There is a gentle, loving side."

"It is the side we put there. Women make this world a living place. Look even at Zeus. He is lecherous and rapacious. His own wife cannot depend upon him. He is always looking over the edge of Olympus for someone to deflower. It made it all the more hypocritical when he condemned Hades for such behavior. And all over that silly girl!"

"I would not like to defend Perserphone, but she learned her silliness at her mother's knee. Who was her father?"

"Some beautiful mortal. The gods have never been able to keep beauty to themselves. We mortals are not only their toys but their temptations, too. Demeter never revealed the father."

"And you, yourself, were moved by Theseus...."

"I should never have told you," Hippolyta spoke in a low voice.

"It made me like you," Ismene protested. "All kings and queens should have a center of love around which their sternness wraps itself."

Hippolyta frowned. "You are rather a poet yourself."

Ismene concentrated on the entertainments the women were providing. She did not want to think of poetry and less of love at this moment. Tieresias was imprisoned, her young Xerxes shut up in a compound like a farm animal, and Hades did not approach her even in her dreams. She suddenly was aware these vivid dreams began since she left the Underworld. Was this the start of her deeper insight? The Oracle of Delphi said one must speak with Hades before one could understand prophecy. The son growing within Ismene would also possess such a gift. Foresight and divinity! Two intertwined parts of a difficult personality. The world might both reward and curse him.

Livia was approaching the banquet table. Her face showed a deep concern.

"The giant of a hundred hands has been seen on the shoreline across the waters."

Hippolyta expressed no deep alarm. "That is no problem, Livia. I have several restless males who might appease him. I believe Zeno is their leader."

Livia's expression did not change. How well she must have practiced since the time the man who loved her was sacrificed, thought Ismene.

Hippolyta arose, "Tomorrow is a festival day. The giant returns for his great feasting. He will have his feast; then we will have ours."

Livia looked towards Ismene in a more revealing manner. This great bulking woman had a soft heart for Zeno. Having met the man, Ismene also wondered how much harm Zeno would actually cause if he could have his Chloe.

"This giant should be dead. In the legends, they promise us a world rid of giants. Why do you not fight him instead of giving precious breeding stock to fill his stomach?"

"It helps my purpose to get these meddling men off my back. Half the women come to me mooning over them. Zeno in particular. He has fixed on Chloe and she on him. He knew the consequences. Yet he fell in love with her."

"You do not sacrifice her." Ismene kept her tone light. She could feel Hippolyta's rising anger.

"And your young Xerxes has been spreading sedition, too," Hippolyta swung around to face her. "In one day, he has told the men about the so-called freedoms citizens of Thebes enjoy under that tyrant, Creon. My spies reported this to me earlier."

Ismene stepped closer, "Xerxes is here as a guest. I will speak with him."

"He is a boy. Like most boys, he does not heed the advice given."

"You would not dare to execute him."

"Who will stop me?"

"I came here to learn from you. Is this what you will teach me?" The entire court watched as the two women locked eyes.

"I thought I was to teach you strength. The strong must be cruel to keep their power."

"We spoke earlier of gentleness."

"We were merely conversing. This giant spurs me into action."

Hippolyta swung around and left the banquet hall, followed by most of her court. Livia remained, her mouth open in amazement.

"I never heard someone so question the queen and live," Livia said at last.

"What did men do to her to make her hate them so?" Ismene wondered out loud.

"Her own father took her virginity when she was nine. We are not to know this story officially, but tongues loosen over the years. Her father then wed her to a man who beat her and used her like a servant. This man was poisoned. No one found the doer of the crime. She took his wealth and moved here to this island, taking with her the many women she had met who were wronged by men. The first rite of becoming an Amazon is the cutting off of one breast."

"Somewhere in her, there is still goodness," Ismene protested.

"She was good to me until someone asked for me in marriage." Livia was biting back her tears.

"I cannot let her kill Xerxes." Ismene was already thinking what she must do to rescue the boy.

"Any more talk with her will bring you a sentence of execution," Livia warned.

"I am not afraid of death. I might even welcome it, considering…" Ismene allowed herself a slight smile.

"No, Ismene. You have another destiny. Death will come to you after many years. If you try to change the fates, Zeus will punish you. He will not give you what you welcome."

"I cannot let Xerxes die, whatever Zeus does to me." Ismene thought of Tieresias's intent in bringing the boy along. To get him out of harm's way, not to expose him to it. She must honor the intent of the prophet. It was time to assess who was her enemy and who was her friend. How would they get off this island should she retrieve Xerxes from the compound? Where would they go? Another journey over the sea. Would Poseidon be her ally again or would he drown them in the waves?

* * *

There were guards posted at her chamber. She bathed in the pool, affecting a casual disdain of the women and their weapons. Looking again into the night, she waited for sleep. Her hope was to find someone in her dreams who could tell her what she must do. Sleep declined to come. She began to pace the length of the chamber, wishing she had stayed in the woodlands under the protection of Artemis. Then she remembered Artemis was also the goddess of the moon. The moon that night was just a knife slice shy of full.

"Artemis," Ismene whispered. "I need your wisdom. If you can come down to me or send me a sign of what I should do, I would be grateful. Can you help me for the sake of Tieresias?"

At that moment, a cloud slid across the bright light of the moon. Ismene stepped back. *Had Artemis denied her?*

"No, Ismene. Try to sleep. Take heart. Tomorrow there will be someone to help you…."

The low humming voice of the goddess sounded in her ears. "I can protect you, but there is someone better than I."

"And Tieresias?"

"Did he ask you for your help?"

"No."

"He has not asked me either."

With that, the cloud moved on, again revealing the silver orb of Artemis. Ismene felt immensely tired. She wrapped herself in Hades's cloak and lay down, remembering suddenly the secret compartment of his cloak. When she left the Kingdom of the Dead, she had put the potion Tieresias had given her to drink in there. It had been unopened, even though he had instructed her to take it when she first met Hades. Now she pulled the small clay bottle out and broke the seal. With one gulp, she swallowed it. Instantly the world around her dropped away, and she stood between the stars in the black of the night.

Below her, at a great distance, she could see the Island of the Amazons, illuminated by a hundred fires. Hippolyta had said her fear was darkness, and the island appeared to sparkle like a bright jewel in the cupped hand of ocean.

Above her was that universe where she had ridden that day with Hades to the bitter end. She thought of his explanation that the Universe was naught but a tapestry of strings which could be torn by an unknowing hand. Now she thought of them as harp strings, plucked and vibrating about her. There was a music to this universe! She could hear it. She could almost see it in the undulating waves of black. It was as beautiful as Hades's deep eyes that swallowed up all light.

Within her, she could hear the singing of her son, accompanying the melody without. It was the voice of a man, not a child, and yet it sounded from her womb. The comfort it gave her was like the lullaby her mother voiced when she was young and frightened. The unborn comforting the woman who carried him.

As though pushed by the winds, pictures flew around her of her life. She saw the happy ones of her childhood, the unhappy ones of her family's deaths, and then the angry ones of Creon.

"And where is Hades?" she shouted into that tunnel of silver light that streamed down from each galaxy. The universe was pitching this way and that. Only she was still. There was a long pause when the music, the wind, the singing stopped. From somewhere, she heard the frantic wings flapping and the snort of fire. Hades on his dragon, flying through the night.

He reached one hand and scooped her up, positioning her in front of him on the great fiery beast. She smelled the funeral herbs and then the sweetness of a million blossoms come from him. She leaned back against his great chest. His lips kissed the back of her neck.

"Where were you?" she asked at last as the dragon fluttered down by that same blue beach and red sea.

He picked her up off the dragon and carried her to a sand dune that felt softer than skin beneath her.

"You do not answer me," she said.

"What answer do you want?" His hands were already touching her stomach, undoing her robes.

"This one," she smiled. "And another....later the other. For now, I am content."

"I cannot linger too long," he sighed, kissing her deeply. "I heard our son singing to me."

She pushed him back lightly. "He was singing to me!"

"You always were difficult," he sighed, and then they did not speak.

* * *

When they had finished making love, Ismene lay in his arms touching his silver skin as though memorizing it.

"It was the potion that brought you. Tieresias must have given it to me when he sent me to you to cause you to fall in love with me."

"A good potion." He smiled a rare smile.

"I never used it in your kingdom. Only tonight. Only because I was desperate for help."

"That was a very loud call you made. You almost woke my wife," Hades growled.

"I woke you. How long have you been asleep that you forgot me?"

"I never forgot you." He gave her an affectionate pinch. "I tried. And then I saw on the walls of my cave-room where you were. I watched every day. You never disappointed me."

"And you should not disappoint me. I need your help. Your dragon must carry us away from the festival tomorrow. They plan to feed Xerxes to the hundred-handed giant."

"Yes, it is Hippolyta's way of keeping order. She used to be a good woman, but now she is a bad queen."

"She said she asked Demeter for Perserphone when your wife was just a girl."

"Demeter was right not to give up her daughter. Selfishness hurts but a few. Power can hurt many."

Suddenly, Ismene did not want to talk about Perserphone.

"You will come with me to get Xerxes…"

"No, I have been forbidden by Zeus."

"You have disobeyed Zeus before!" She sat up indignantly.

"I was placed in the Underworld for disobeying Zeus…."

Ismene knew his deep sorrow. She swallowed her words of reproach. Their time was almost at an end.

"Can you fly me back to the Island of the Amazons?"

"Yes, my love. That much, Zeus will not forbid," Hades sighed. He kissed her long and hard. "You are no longer the child I picked up at the entrance to my kingdom...."

"Are you happy about your son?"

Hades nodded.

"And Perserphone..."

"She dares not complain. In her time on the earth, she was untrue to me. She carries her own child."

* * *

The flight back to the Island of the Amazons was quiet. Ismene rode in front of Hades; his head rested heavily on her shoulder. She felt, at that moment, between sleep and wakefulness, balanced carefully between the two states. Her problem had not been solved, but Artemis told her help would come in the morning. The night had been posited with other concerns. It proved to her Hades loved her. It also proved to her that their time together would always be stolen between the paths they both must take.

The dragon made a quiet descent onto the terrace. Ismene allowed herself the final pleasure of having Hades lift her off.

"Take care of our son," he spoke solemnly, then disarmed her by smiling and kissing her as though he were off for only a few hours. The dragon bore him back into the heavens.

Ismene lay in the comfort of his cloak and fell asleep instantly.

* * *

"Wake up, Princess. It is festival day." Hippolyta herself was shaking Ismene awake.

"Did I oversleep?"

"Yes, you missed the entrance of the great giant. We give him a parade when he comes, and then throw him a cow or two to stave off his hunger until the Great Eating."

There was food laid out for Ismene. Hippolyta sat beside her as she ate, braiding the long blonde hair of the Princess.

"You spoke harshly to me last night," Hippolyta said at last.

"I spoke truth to you. If truth is harsh, I must speak that way." Ismene took the queen's hand. "You were kind to me at first. I am unprepared for this cruelty to others who do no more than care for someone."

"I saw your father once. You have his softness," Hippolyta replied in return, disengaging her hand. "And your mother's strange looks..."

"I will always miss my parents. Now especially. I used to look at them with a child's eyes of love, but now that I am going to be a parent, I see how truly rare their qualities were."

"Incest," Hippolyta curled her lip.

"No more, it seems, than our gods indulge in. Is not Hera the sister of Zeus as well as his wife?"

"We hold the gods to a different standard." Hippolyta tapped Ismene's arm.

"But we should not hold them to a different standard, unless it is a better standard," Ismene said. In her heart, she remembered last night where Hades's infidelity was matched by that of Perserphone.

"You said we might fight the giant rather than appease him...."

Ismene watched Hippolyta's face shift from a hard mask into concern. "I would like to hear your plan."

"I did not have a plan. But together—all of us—can try to devise one." Was this the help Artemis promised? From the very person who had wanted to kill Xerxes?

"I thought about what you said. I have jealous motives for wanting Zeno dead. Chloe is dearly beloved by me...." The queen was walking on dangerous territory now, confessing her lust for one of her subjects.

"And Chloe? Should she not be allowed to choose?"

"She has chosen. Before I came to your chamber, I asked for her choice....she chose me."

Ismene did not ask if it was an honest choice. She remembered Livia's fear of Hippolyta. Perhaps Chloe chose Hippolyta in a hope to spare Zeno's life. But then, the queen was quite a beautiful woman. Maybe the choice was authentic.

"Let us think. How does the festival work?"

"The giant is set on a great stool in the center of the arena. We bring in a line of men, chained. As we unfetter them one by one, the giant reaches out and catches one. He then eats the victim, and the next is presented. When it is over, we go off to our own feasting."

"And this is performed in a precise order?"

"Yes."

Ismene thought of the plays she had seen in the theater in her city, where often a slight of hand would fool a buffoon who saw what he wished to see.

"Does the giant eat them in a hurry?"

"The first few. After that, he slows down and chews...."

"We could have a man made from old skins and filled with a poison....this man would be fettered with the real men. The giant could then..."

Hippolyta smiled, "The giant is notoriously bad-sighted."

"I do not think we need the others." Ismene clapped her hands. "There is the plan."

"But the others must pretend as though their deaths were near," Hippolyta added. "The giant has a good sense of smell, and he likes the aroma of dying."

* * *

The arena was filled with subjects of the Island of Amazon , all dressed in bright tunics of red and green. A stool that was higher than a large hill was set in the center of the arena.

Ismene stood beside Xerxes, third in the line of fettered men.

"Tell everyone the minute the giant eats the first victim to stay out of the way. Go as far to the side of the area as you can. This monster has a hundred hands that will be clutching and reaching. The poison is painful, quick, and will make him very angry before it kills him."

"The queen has consented to this?" Xerxes asked.

"She helped me think of it," Ismene replied.

"Then I think it is a false plan."

"I will stake my life on it. I will join the line of fettered victims," Ismene took up the challenge.

"No, Princess. Your life is marked as special. You cannot sacrifice your life for us," Xerxes protested.

"I will," Ismene said, turning to the guard. "Put the chains on me."

The guard looked at her in surprise and then placed the heavy chains around her ankles. At that moment, the giant appeared. He had the look of weathered rocks. His skin was bumpy and mottled. From his powerful arms, extended fifty hands on the right, and fifty on the left. He was completely nude with drool running continually from his mouth. When he saw the crowd, he did not bow, but rather sat immediately on the great stool. The crowd cheered.

Ismene looked to the first man. It was Zeno! Where was the man made of skins and filled with a poison! Her eyes went to the dais where Hippolyta was sitting. Xerxes was correct. The plan was a false one.

Livia came running over to Ismene. "Princess, what is this? You should be joining the queen now." Livia was confused.

"I cannot. As you see, I am about to die with the others." Ismene wanted to say more, but a guard pushed Livia away.

"No, Princess!" Livia called. The queen was raising her arm to gesture to the giant that the prisoners were coming out.

In a second, Livia had run across the arena. The giant leaned down and scooped her up without a thought, swallowing her in one gulp.

Hippolyta rose in horror. "A mistake!" she cried, but too late. The crowd was suddenly angry. Livia had been a favorite of many of the women for her loyalty.

"Citizens, a mistake," Hippolyta cried out again.

Suddenly, a young woman rose from behind the queen.

"Chloe!" Zeno called.

"You told us this time would be a sham." Chloe pushed Hippolyta. "Zeno would be safe."

At that moment, Ismene saw a dagger flash. Hippolyta slumped against the slender form of the woman.

"Here, giant, is your first victim!" Chloe pushed the body over the side of the dais. The giant looked in bewilderment and then reached down. His hundred hands were twitching with expectation as he picked up the queen, stuffing her in his mouth.

"We are doomed," Xerxes moaned. Just at that moment, the giant stumbled, angrily pulling at his tongue.

"I do not think we are doomed," Ismene said slowly.

The giant gagged and retched, but he could not dislodge the body of the queen from his mouth.

The crowd came to their feet, yelling chaotically. The giant turned his hands, trying to grab at them. Then he fell with a *thud*. There was a long silence. The queen, herself, crawled from his mouth.

"This giant is no more. The legends have been corrected. Cut open his stomach, and I believe you will find Livia….but quickly."

Livia was pulled out, to the joy of the citizens.

The men were released and brought to the queen who looked each of them in the eye before she said, "I pardon you. It is a wise queen who will try to make friends of her enemies."

The men knelt before her.

"And Zeno…" Hippolyta took his hands to raise him up. "Chloe is waiting for you."

Ismene stood with Xerxes until Hippolyta noticed her, "Your plan was good, Ismene, but the giant might not have been fooled by so artificial a figure as a man of skins. It was necessary for me to do some revisions. I had poison in my hand, which I poured down the giant's throat. Then I hung on for dear life to his snaggly tooth."

With a cry, Ismene hugged and kissed her.

"You were willing to die with your friend here. I think I have nothing to teach you, while you had much to teach me," Hippolyta laughed.

"I am…I am…"

"Princess, what is it?"

"I am happy, Hippolyta, but I must go lie down. My child is coming!" Ismene shouted.

* * *

The child lay in her arms, silver-skinned and eyes containing the whole of darkness. Xerxes stood at a distance, pale and worried. Hippolyta helped deliver the baby. She took a cloth herself and washed away the blood, cutting the cord that bound the son to the mother.

"What do you name him?"

"I have no name. It is for his father to decide the name."

The sucking of the boy at her breast filled her with peace.

"He looks like his father," Hippolyta remarked, "from what I have seen of statues in the temple."

"He is the very image," Ismene agreed, "and when he is weaned I must take him to Hades; unless, of course, Hades would like to come for him." She remembered last night at the edge of the universe.

"You will be leaving us," Hippolyta put an arm around Xerxes's shoulder.

"Soon. Can you ask Poseidon to be gentle with his waters on that day?"

* * *

The child lived at the palace, breaking the ban on males residing there. Ismene used to tease Hippolyta that she would have a husband next.

"I will have a husband when Zeus is faithful to Hera for a moon," Hippolyta would reply.

Xerxes, by this time, had learned the skills of a warrior. He was impatient for the journey home.

"I want to show Tieresias what I have learned...," he bragged. Ismene did not tell him that Tieresias had been imprisoned and might even be dead by the time they arrived.

The night before they were to leave, there was a great celebration. The men left the compound and came to the palace to sleep with the women, and contrary to past times, Hippolyta said they might stay the evening out. When the world was quiet, Ismene held her baby close, filled with sorrow that she must part from him.

A rustle of the leaves was heard. Standing before her was Hades.
"Let me see him," he spoke gently. She slipped the child into his arms.
"I did not name him," she whispered.
"I know. I watch you...." His eyes lingered on hers.
"Did Perserphone have her child?"
"Yes, a girl. Just as pretty and slippery as her mother."
"They can grow together."
"That the laughter of children will ring through the Kingdom of Death. It is a difficult concept, even for me," Hades said.
Ismene felt the chill of parting already.
"Are you pleased?"
Hades looked into her eyes. She saw the flash of tears in his own. Even the blackness could not hide them.
"Beloved..." she said.
"But I have come to take you home, myself. And then return to my kingdom. My dragon is down in the meadow."
"Xerxes will get to ride a dragon!"
"And I..." Hades put the sleeping infant down gently, "will have this night with you."

* * *

The eyrie seemed deserted when she first arrived, but then memories animated it. Xerxes immediately set about gathering fruits for them to eat. Ismene was still elated from her night with Hades and the ride home. Her arms missed the feel of her child, and then the emptiness drained over her.
"A sad homecoming," she said out loud. "No one to greet me."
The next day, she made her way down the hillside over Xerxes's protests to the palace.
"I beg audience with King Creon," she demanded of the soldier loitering at the gate.
"The king has died of old battle wounds. We are in mourning."
"And Tieresias?" She started at the news.
"Tieresias is consulting with the citizens."
"They did not kill him?"

"No, lady. Creon only held him, hoping to lure Princess Ismene here. The king thought she might attempt to plead for the prophet's release."

"The king was correct..." Ismene smiled in spite of herself. Tieresias was safe.

"Tell the prophet that his eyrie is home to a returning bird," she said, and ran up the cliffs. It was twilight when she finally heard the slow walk of the old man.

Xerxes set a fire and then went off to sleep under the stars. He insisted that Ismene should have her moment with Tieresias.

"Your son..."

She thrilled at his voice, "Is with his father. As am I..."

"At least I will not have to ask the birds to bury me."

When she turned, she saw no more than bones covered by old skin. "Creon did this!" she cried.

"No. Time did this." He shook his head slowly. "Xerxes is to be the new king. I arranged today with the nobles that your little charge should take the crown. No one is better suited, except yourself."

Ismene felt happy. "I can stay here with you."

"I am leaving...."

"Where would you go in this world?"

"Nowhere...In this world. I will join your son, your family. I will even join Creon."

"And I?"

He came close to her. "Listen to me, Ismene. When I die, take my skin, put it over yourself. You will fill it. My blind eyes will see again. You must be the voice of truth. Xerxes needs your truth to rule his land."

"But you..."

"You are ready. Remember that day you fled Creon?"

She thought of how she believed he could shelter her.

"I sent you on your way. The gifts were always there to be opened. Now, you have gifts to give others."

His voice was weak. "I was only waiting for your return."

She turned from him to the fire. "Is it different than you thought, when death finally comes?"

121

"It is like the fire I have always feared and always needed. I can put my hand in it at last...." And so saying, he put his fingers forward towards the red tongue of heat.

"Yes," she said. She saw ahead where one day she would cross the Styx to meet her son, grown tall and proud. Like the nesting bird, the eyrie gave her rest before the flight.

EPILOGUE

Xerxes was made king. The youngest king that Thebes had seen. Ismene attended his council meetings, sharing her wisdom with the citizens of the city. She always thought of what Tieresias would do. Then one night, Tieresias came to her in a dream and scolded her, "Stop thinking of my thoughts. Think your own."

Hades flew in on his dragon when she felt most alone. He brought their son, whom he named Philo. The boy always looked at her with shining eyes as though the black had been polished.

"It is your light that glows there," Hades told her. "Your beauty."

As she grew older, she went into the city less and less. Finally, she stayed in the eyrie, looking out with eyes that saw both ahead and behind. Her adventures of the past became legends. Once in a while, when Xerxes came to visit, he told her the latest version. They laughed together over it.

On the wall of her seeing-room in the secret cave, she watched Hippolyta grow old alone. She saw Perserphone's daughter and Philo become sister and brother in thought. She watched Perserphone grow into a serious queen. On the last day of her life, she dressed herself in blue robes and braided her silver hair as though she were a maiden going to a wedding. When she reached the Netherworld, she knew Hades would be waiting for her.

THE END

Printed in the United States
113706LV00003B/169/A